The Disgrace of Colonel Caine

Mickey J. "Mike" Martin

This book is a work of fiction. Any form of reference to real people, events, establishments, organizations, or locales is intended only to add a sense of authenticity.   All other characters and dialogue have been drawn from the author's imagination and are not to be construed as real.

ISBN 9781737140610 — Hardback (Large Print)
ISBN 9781737140627 — Paperback (Large Print)
ISBN 9781737140634 — EPUB
LCCN: 2022902003

****

The Disgrace of Colonel Caine

CONTENTS

*****

— 1 —

SETTLER CAINE

WHEN THE FEDERAL GOVERNMENT made land in the Oklahoma Indian Territory available for outside settlement, there was an immediate swell of interest. The region grew as people flocked to it, and it was obvious that even more growth was likely in the future. Opportunity seekers of all persuasions began coming and going at will, every one of them intent upon finding a way to capitalize on this mass emigration. Some showed up with the intention of investing in town lots or farm properties that could be resold for a higher price, while others showed up planning to start new lives and stay for the long haul. For all of them, land in the territory had proven to be an irresistible lure.

Among the newcomers who showed up in the territory during these heady days was a man by the name of George Jackson Caine, who arrived in 1906 from Van Buren, Arkansas, the county seat of Crawford County, which is several hours west of Little Rock and close to Fort Smith in Sebastian County. His father, a poor but morally upstanding farmer by the name of David Paul Caine, was also a combination church elder and lay preacher. Born on February 20, 1882, George's middle name was given to him in memory of

Civil War hero General Thomas "Stonewall" Jackson. Many sons of the South received their first or middle name in this same way, which is one reason why Jackson is a common name in southern states.

George Caine knew no more than the unavoidable minimum about the Creek Indians whose land had become available, and he didn't care to know any more than what he already knew. He looked down on all non-white racial and ethnic groups, based on the assumption that all of them were inferior to his own. His greatest scorn was reserved for black people, but the Indians who once owned the land he intended to settle on and who were so numerous in the territory came in a close second.

Truth be known, Caine was contemptuous of most everyone but himself, including members of his own race. He was a highly self-focused young man, a person so intent on his own interests and pursuits that he barely noticed anyone else's needs, wants, or preferences. He didn't know much about his new surroundings, but he figured that what he did know would be more than enough to enable him to achieve the overall aim that had drawn him to the territory from his birthplace in Arkansas.

Caine had no doubt about why he wanted to settle in a location as remote as the new Indian Territory town of Hoffman: He intended to take full advantage of the low-cost land that was available there. He took for granted that the bountiful returns earned from the rich farmland he intended to buy would make him an independently wealthy man, someone who would never have to work for anyone else. His goal was to accumulate wealth through the ownership of property, and, day in and day out, he dreamt of nothing else.

George had grown sick of living like his father, who stayed as poor as a church mouse no matter how many hours of hard labor he put in on his farm. His father's acquaintances considered him a decent and principled man, but that hadn't mattered much to George. He knew people had high regard for his father, but the problem he had with his old man was that hard labor seemed to be all he knew, and hard work out on the farm was what he had demanded of his son. Because he worked hard himself, his father expected George to do likewise. Knowing that the great majority of men in the country made their living by farming, he thought it was his duty to make sure his son became used to hard work. He wanted George to work as long and as hard each day as he did himself.

George, though, was nothing like his father; he was something of a swell, a person who had a very high opinion of himself. He saw the world through his own lens, and he was not amenable to following orders, no matter who issued them, his father or anyone else, whether they were reasonable or not. As soon as he thought he had learned enough from his father to make a go of it on his own, that's exactly what he chose to do. He had no intention of working for anyone but himself, ever again.

He and his father had clashed over their conflicting attitudes toward work, just as they had over many other things. Their differences went far beyond George's reluctance to do his best out on the farm, due to their viewing the world in vastly divergent manners. In many ways, father and son were as unalike as night and day, and, in the end, it all boiled down to differences in values. George was nothing at all like his highly principled father.

When his father did not have him up to his neck laboring on the family farm, George had a habit of riding into Fort Smith in search of good times, and good times, by his definition, always meant a combination of chasing after girls, drinking, or gambling. He seldom had enough money to do the latter, so he made up for it by doing as much as possible of the former. Like most young men, the pursuit of feminine companionship was always high on his agenda, but George had become a skirt-chaser of the worst kind.

On those occasions when he didn't have enough cash in hand to do as he pleased in town, he'd borrow money from one or another of his drinking buddies. Because they were interested in the same things, he and his friends backed one another up when they could. They had become known for always being able to find a way to hang one on and pick up any girls who were interested in having a good time. George was a good-looking, virile, energetic, young man, which meant that he was usually able to find someone, and he enjoyed the hunt as much as he enjoyed the catch.

Through their acquaintance with his father, George knew sets of parents who felt okay with his going out with their daughters. Because they had high esteem for Caine senior, they figured Caine junior, even though he was known to be something of a hell raiser, would also become a good man one day. They had no way of knowing how dead wrong they were, or that George, even if he had realized the extent to which he had benefitted from his father's sterling reputation, would have done exactly what he wanted to do, regardless of the effect it had on anyone else, including his father. That's just the way he was.

Every time he came home drunk, bitter arguments broke out between George and his father. Like any dedicated parent, he hoped to persuade his son to grow up and behave like a responsible adult, which was why he did everything he could to protect his son and family's reputations. As it turned out, though, nothing he said or did was enough to tear George away from the habits that kept getting him into trouble.

As George grew older, he became even more irresponsible, not less. He got into some sort of trouble or came home drunk almost every time he went into town. Reckless behavior had become a way of life for him, and word of every entanglement he got into eventually got back to his father.

Bitter argumentation between them grew in intensity with every month that passed, until, finally, neither one of them could take it anymore. If George had not decided to pack up and leave of his own accord, his father would have booted him out the door; their relationship had become that intolerable.

The problem with the intangible concept of honor, George had concluded, was that it could not be measured, nor could it be used to buy property, put good food on the table, or purchase fine clothing to wear. Buying and enjoying good things in life required money, and that's what he intended to have. Building up a personal estate had become his entire focus of attention. He would do it, too, he had decided, if not in one way, then in another. He had been willing to plow fields with his father for a while, but only for a while. Now that he was out on his own, it was time to make something happen. Materialistic in the extreme, he had made up his mind; he would do whatever was needed to achieve the standing he thought he deserved. He left home determined to find something better than a sweat-of-the-brow way of making a living.

— 2 —

COLONEL
GEORGE JACKSON CAINE

GEORGE CAINE SHOWED UP in the Indian Territory under what those who lived in the area around where he bought land soon came to believe were less than decent and honorable circumstances, even though not a one of them ever learned what those circumstance might have been. Gossip had it that he left Arkansas in the middle of the night and in an unusual hurry, but this comment lost traction when no way to substantiate it could be found.

More rumors began to circulate about Caine as well, one of them being that he had been "personally acquainted with some widely known outlaws in the Territory" and that he had "once run with some notorious gang members." Not a word of this could be proven, but talk of this kind made his new Indian, black, and white neighbors wary of him from the beginning. They wanted to know more about him, but because he looked to be a person who wouldn't appreciate any probing into his past no one was willing to push for details.

Due to his rigid military-like bearing and combative demeanor and because it made some-thing of a clever play on his middle name, not long after his arrival in the territory a few of Caine's neighbors and acquaintances began referring to him behind his back as "The Colonel." They used the term as a not-so-subtle jab against his aggressive personality, but it never occurred to him that the nickname started as a pejorative. Once he heard it and had time to think it over, he got a kick out of the moniker; in fact, he liked it so much that he started using it himself. "They call me Colonel," he began saying to people he met, "so you call me that, too." Soon, everybody in the area began referring to him as *The Colonel*, even though he had no military experience at all. Assigning nicknames to others was common throughout the Territory, and anyone who was considered somebody by anybody seemed to have had one.

George was, from the outset, something of an intimidating figure among his hard-working neighbors, not due to any overt effort on his part to appear that way but due to his quirks, mannerisms, and overall appearance. Some of his neighbors, truth be known, felt unsettled in his presence.

His light blue-gray eyes were so penetrating that he seemed to look straight through a person, and he had a way of staring at people with a faint grin until they felt compelled to turn away. Despite the grin, he didn't laugh aloud very often, even when someone told a good joke or a story that brought out laughter from others.

More unusual characteristics came into play when Caine interacted with others, as if those already mentioned weren't enough to make some neighbors hesitant.   One of the most unusual things about him was that, when he spoke to people, he unknowingly assumed a stance that came across as threatening.   Instead of addressing a person straight on, he would turn about 45 degrees to one side as he faced them, put one foot ahead of the other, and lean back a bit.   With his knees slightly bent, he would keep his left hand a little forward of his torso and his right hand a little behind it.   Then, as he spoke, he had a habit of clenching, releasing, and re-clinching his hands into fists.   These tics combined to produce a combative look, as if he were bracing for a fight. He wasn't, though; it was a natural posture that he didn't even think about, no matter what mood he happened to be in.   It was just the way he was, but it appeared threatening, anyway.   Because no one knew what to make of this behavior, it made even more people uneasy around him.

Due to all the talk that was circulating, neighbors continued to refrain from asking George questions about where he came from or why he had landed in their midst.   They wanted to know, but they weren't about to ask.   Plus, since more than a few of them had moved to their out-of-the-way location to put behind questionable pasts of their own, no one considered insisting on detailed answers to specific questions. After a while, George Caine blended well enough into his new surroundings to be as well accepted as anyone else. Before long, no one had anything further to say about his former life, whatever it might have been.

Although it never became clear what secrets Caine wanted to hide, what could not be hidden was that he arrived in the area with an attractive, unusually quiet, and notably pregnant young wife. That, of course, was in no way remarkable, since it was common for people in the area to marry young and have a lot of children, but what did raise a lot of eyebrows was that he showed up with enough hard money in hand to pay cash for the forty-acre farm he bought from a freedman who had decided to move to Tulsa to live closer to his family. In a location where most farmers and ranchers, whether they were new to the area or already proven, tended to be cash poor, it was uncommon for a young farmer to pay for a parcel of land up front.

Because almost every one of his neighbors had had to take out one or more loans to finance farmland or equipment or mules or what have you, it was noticeable—and remarkable—that he had not. Overnight it became common knowledge that he had transferred to J. M. Kinyon, one of the two so-called *sole agents* of the Hoffman Townsite and Realty Company, enough cash money to buy, without taking out a mortgage, what everyone described as "nigger Sanderson's old farm up on the north side of town, off the state highway between Henryetta and Checotah; you know the one."

It was in no way illegal or underhanded for Caine to pay up front for his farm, but it was impossible for people not to wonder how a man as young as he was could have come by that much ready money. All his neighbors knew was that his was not a typical purchase. To them, it was yet another reason to consider him unusual. It also raised a whole new series of questions for which there were no ready answers.

The flurry of unanswerable questions combined with his unusual characteristics to make George Caine a local mystery. In short order after he arrived in the settlement, he was labeled a dodgy and questionable individual. It didn't surprise anyone that he hadn't volunteered much personal information, since many of them were not too voluble about themselves, either. Even so, people tended to shy away from what they didn't understand, and that was how many of his neighbors reacted toward him—Indians, blacks, and whites alike.

It also quickly became clear to everyone that Caine was every bit as testy and combative as he appeared, and that it wasn't good to start going around and around with him about anything, trivial or not. It was best to steer clear of him, his neighbors soon decided, so most of them interacted with him only when they had to and left it at that.

It wasn't long before some of the locals began to speak of him among themselves as "an unfriendly, surly, and excessively aggressive sonofabitch," a man who for one reason or another behaved as if he "bore some sort of grudge against the whole damned world." Pointless surliness was his natural state, but no one ever learned why. The only thing people learned for certain about him was that he wasn't someone to quibble with face-to-face.

The Caines avoided voluntary social events, and they engaged in no more contact with others than the minimum necessary to conduct essential activities, such as trading for groceries, buying farm supplies like equipment and livestock, and picking up mail. Like his neighbors, Caine had to focus on dealing with the mundane matters that were associated with trying to make a living off the Oklahoma farmland he'd bought. Some of his neighbors surmised that after their baby boy died during childbirth, Caine and his wife just wanted to keep to themselves for a while, perhaps because that was their way of grieving.

George Caine was most definitely harder to deal with than most of his contemporaries, not only due to his pugnaciousness but also because other personal quirks contributed to his already highly unusual mystique. One of his quirks, for example, was that he rarely ever washed his hair, since he believed that too much washing would make it grow thinner as he aged.

"Now, wasn't that silly?" one neighbor remembered having once remarked to another one morning as they stood beside a barnyard gate, talking about Caine's peculiarities, according to the father of one of my sources of information: "Nearly ever body washed his hair once in a while, even back in them days." This was an inconsequential matter, but it was during conversations as ordinary as this that the Colonel's reputation for being as strange as he was intimidating continued to grow as months and years passed by.

— 3 —

THE COLONEL
FAILS AS A FARMER

AFTER ONLY FIVE YEARS of trying to make a living by raising crops on his own plot of Indian Territory farmland, it became clear to everyone, especially to the Colonel himself, that farming was never going to be his calling in life. To begin with, he clearly didn't have much of a knack for it, and, besides that, it had not taken long for him to learn that dry land farming, especially without his father's guidance, was a hell of a lot tougher way of making a living than he thought it was going to be. Working alone had turned out to be just as hard and sweaty as working with his father. Thankfully, though, he thought to himself, it had been much less aggravating.

One year the weather was so dry that his corn and cotton dried up in their fields. The next year, weevils, grasshoppers, and other pests destroyed so much of what he planted that the rest wasn't worth harvesting. In other years, commodity prices dropped too low to turn a reasonable profit, despite his having managed to pull off some decent yields.

Once things started to go downhill out on his place, the stash of money he still had on hand from wherever he had gotten what he came in with quickly began to disappear. A lot was going out each year, but not too much was coming back in. It had become obvious that, if things kept going the way they were, it wouldn't be long before he'd be flat broke.

Then, right in the middle of a season during which his farming operation was teetering on the brink of going under, his home life also took a terrible turn for the worse. After contracting an illness that their country doctor had been unable to accurately diagnose or properly treat, his attractive young wife got sick and, shortly thereafter, abruptly died.

Cemetery records show that it wasn't uncommon during the early 1900s for a spouse or child to die at a young age, particularly out in the territory, with the availability of good medical care being as poor as it was, but Caine's wife's passing, coming as it did when he was on the verge of losing his means of earning a livelihood, had to have been an especially difficult blow. Having lost a son during childbirth and then his wife soon after that brought about a low point in the Colonel's life, in the same way that it would have for anyone.

After his wife passed, the Colonel had to deal with the misery of loneliness, on top of all of his other problems. *Is there no damned way*, he grumbled to himself, *that I can get ahead in this miserable world!* To him, his situation was maddening. Firmly convinced that not a thing that had happened was any fault of his own, and he grew increasingly agitated.

Blaming his problems on everything and everybody but himself, he became more irascible with every week that passed.

When his farming operation finally went into the red and failed miserably not too long thereafter, he tried to hang on to his land by earning as much as he could through engaging in such diverse side activities as trading in livestock and farm implements, operating a truck garden, doing various piecework jobs, and selling game he killed and fish he caught out of the nearby Deep Fork River bottom.   When these catch-as-catch-can ways of getting by proved to be insufficient, he had no choice but to give up on any though of staying out on his farm and put his property up for sale.   After selling out for much less than he'd paid, he left behind his rural land on the north side of town and moved into Hoffman proper.   What he was going to do when he got there, he had absolutely no idea.

— 4 —

FROM COUNTRY MAN
TO TOWN MAN

NOT LONG AFTER he gave up on being a "country man" to become a "town man," as locals referred to such a move at the time, the Colonel found himself caught up in a desperate search for a new way to make a living. He could read and write well enough to get by, but not much better than that. Neither did he have any readily marketable skills. Positions for laborers were available, but he was determined to stay as far away as possible from any more of that kind of work. He had already done all the hard labor he intended to do, first during his years as his father's peon and then on his own farm.

Before long, Caine found himself between yet another rock and hard spot. Earning a good living in town, he had discovered, had turned out to be just as tough as getting by out on his farm. Cursing his bad luck, he knew he had to do something soon, since it was clear that his money wasn't going to last forever. He had had to sell his farmland at a loss, and, after paying off his debts, there wasn't as much left as he expected.

In Hoffman, job pickings were slim for any man who was unwilling to work hard. There weren't many jobs of the leisurely kind to be had, if there were any at all. In the early 1900s, about 80 percent of the workforce was employed in farming, and farming, by definition, meant arduous work. Without a doubt, Caine had to have feared that his dream of running his own business and building up an estate through owning property would never be realized.

In the words of an old man whose parents had been long-term residents of Hoffman, "My dad told me that Caine lived for a while in the old Hunter house, in a room he rented from Jim Hunter while he was scramblin' around lookin' for some way to make an easy livin'. The house was a double-story building, and he lived in one of them three or four upstairs rooms. It was up on the east side of the north Main Street and east of the schoolhouse, as you headed away from the center of town in the direction of Tulsa. This was between 1911 and 1913, somewhere around in there. Different people rented them rooms at different times, some livin' upstairs and some livin' downstairs. Later, that property was bought by old lady Herring, who passed away. Everbody in Hoffman know'd who Caine was, since he wasn't nothin' but a good-for-nothing. Dad told me all about him, and they's newspaper articles about some of the stuff he got into later."

In any case, what mattered most to Caine at that point was not where he had to live after moving into town but that he sure as hell wanted to avoid having to do any more hard and sweaty work. That's what he moved into town to avoid.   For him, farming had dropped off the list; it was completely behind him.   It never occurred to him that he hadn't failed at farming after giving it his best efforts; he'd failed, frankly, because he was no good at it, being neither determined nor diligent enough be successful. There's a big difference.

Caine was a crafty and intelligent man, but he had too little education to earn a living in a profession like bookkeeping or teaching, and he had never held a steady wage-paying or salaried job. Farming was the only work he had ever done, first for his father and then on his own. His obvious problem after showing up in Hoffman proper was that he didn't have a single clue what he was going to do, once he was there. His having originally moved into the area thinking that dry land farming was going to be a sure way to earn good income and build up a holding of property proved, if it proved nothing else, that he had an exceptionally poor understanding of his own skills and aptitudes and abilities.

— 5 —

CAINE, THE
RELUCTANT BARBER

THE COLONEL'S FIRST RESIDENCE in Hoffman was indeed a rental in a business called The Hunter House, which advertised *a room and an all-you-can-eat home cooked meal for $1 per night.* Until the Hunter family took it over, it had been known as Knight's Hotel, the first hotel ever built in Hoffman. It was built by a man by the name of Harold Knight, who arrived on the scene out of Missouri. The old two-story building fronted the east side of Main Street, which was the in-town stretch of the primary north and south county road that ran through the middle of town. It would have to do, thought the Colonel, until he got a better handle on things.

Not long after he got situated at the boarding house, George learned that Harmony's Barbershop, the only barbershop in town, had a vacant chair. The shop was situated within walking distance to the north of Harmony's Store on the west side of Main Street, just north of east-west running Fourth Street. It was owned and leased out by John David Harmony, a well-known and prosperous landholder and merchant who owned other going concerns as well as various lease and rental properties around town.

Reluctantly, he decided to apply for the job, but not because he was interested in barbering. He applied because it was the only open position that did not involve hard physical labor.

When he inquired about the possibility of making a job change from farming to barbering, J. D. Harmony stoutly encouraged his interest. It made sense for Harmony to urge him on, since such a career move on Caine's part meant that he would begin to receive double monthly space rental payments from his shop instead of only one. His shop was just a large, blank, wide-open room in a building that faced Main Street, a room that was devoid of any personality at all. Had there been enough business to justify them, Harmony could have added a dozen more barbering chairs. Cautious study would have shown that there might not be enough for even one additional chair, but he carefully avoided getting into all of that.

Old man Harmony was wealthy enough to have been able to cover the cost of building a new grammar school for the community out of his own pocket, back when the old one burned down. Once the new facility was constructed on the same foundation as the old, all local taxpayers had to do to keep the school up and running was pay teacher salaries and keep up the building. For residents of the town of Hoffman, and especially for parents raising children, Harmony's generosity had been a civic windfall.

Harmony, as would be imagined, was much revered and exceptionally well liked in Hoffman and throughout the surrounding area, since not too many other residents would have been willing to make such a grand gesture as building a public schoolhouse, even if they could have afforded to do so. For reasons such as this, Harmony was considered a cornerstone of Hoffman, and he was highly respected for his civic-minded largess.

Using a part of his remaining cash, Caine jumped at the chance to pay in advance for a six-month lease on the chair space that was open at the barbershop. Harold Upshaw, the man who leased the other chair, was upset over the new arrangement, but there wasn't much he could do about it, since Mr. Harmony owned the shop and the space within it was his to rent out as he saw fit.

As would be expected, Upshaw was concerned about holding on to his existing customers, as he had at once doubted that there would be enough barbering business in Hoffman to share with anyone. In an area where common practice was for farmers and ranchers to have their hair cut at home by their wives or mothers or daughters, he had managed to build up enough of a clientele to make a living, and, understandably, he wanted to hang on to every customer he had.

George Caine didn't know the first thing about barbering, but that was no barrier to entering the trade. At the time, barbering was a skill learned through hands-on practice; all that mattered was whether a man could cut hair well enough to draw in a sufficient number of new and repeat customers to make a living. If he did, he would get by; if he didn't, he would go broke. Employment in the trade was as uncomplicated as that.

Few people made appointments for haircuts or shaves, which meant that most business was conducted on a walk-in basis. Upshaw, as the holder of the shop's first chair, expected to get by on the income earned from his established clients, while the Colonel, of course, would have to draw in new customers of his own. Upshaw made it even harder for Caine to get started by insisting on reserving first right to any customer who showed up at the shop, claiming that his holding the first chair gave him that right.

Upshaw's take on their business arrangement was that customers ought to be bumped to Caine's chair only when his own wasn't occupied. That was only fair, he argued, in view of how he had had to struggle for years to build up a decent client base. He had regular customers, and the last thing he wanted to do was to turn them over to someone else. He didn't have anything against the Colonel, but he didn't think a new man had any right to succeed at his personal expense. Caine, he was convinced, should have to build up his own clientele, in the same way he had.   That, from his perspective, was the only reason-able way to move ahead.

It didn't take long for the Colonel to understand that he had locked himself into a business arrange-ment that worked out well for Mr. Harmony and for Harold Upshaw but put him in an untenable position. There had never been enough business to justify em-ploying a second barber.   Worse still, new customers who were bumped to his chair learned after only one cutting and a quick glance in a mirror to avoid him at all costs during their next visit.   Even if he had been adept enough to hang on to some of the customers whose hair he cut, so few ended up in his chair that it would never have been possible for him to earn a de-cent living.

When the combination of the way too high monthly payments on the long-term lease agreement he signed at the urging of the slick negotiating Har-mony and his own monthly living expenses began to eat up his savings at an alarming rate, George Caine realized that he couldn't allow things to go on as they were.   Something had to be done, and it had to be done *fast*.

So, once again, there he was, wrapped up in yet another business venture in which more money was going out every month than coming in.   He had al-ready failed at farming, and now he was on the brink of failing as a barber.   For a man with his elevated level of ambition, he had to have been extremely aggravated about his predicament.

— 6 —

BIDING TIME, IN SEARCH OF A WAY UP

THE COLONEL HAD NO IDEA how he was going to make it happen, but he was just as determined as ever to become a wealthy man.   Even during his darkest moments, he never lost sight of the overall goal that had motivated him to move to the Indian Territory back in 1906, which was his dream of accumulating personal wealth through the ownership of property and running a business of his own. His only problem was that he had not yet figured out how he was going to do it.

It didn't even register with him that he had no business-related insight, foresight, or skills of any kind.   To him, all that mattered was that he knew what he wanted to do, that he was determined to do it, and that he had no intention of ever giving up.   He was frustrated, but only for the moment.   His ship had not come in yet, but it would.   He had a clear goal; he just had not latched on to a workable way of getting after it.   He would get there, he figured, if he kept on searching.

Come hell or high water, he swore to himself, *I'm going to get where I want to be, no matter what I have to do to make it happen.*   Through gritted teeth, he vowed that he would never give up the hunt. *I may have failed as a farmer and I might be on the verge of failing as a barber,* he told himself, *but I'm never going to give up on reaching my overall goal.* He didn't, either; he remained as ambitious as ever.

Opportunists like George Caine were common in the Indian Territory during the early 1900s, and every one of them had the same thing in mind as him: To make as much as possible, as quickly as possible, and as easily as possible. Most people arrived in the area willing to *work hard*, but men of their kind showed up wanting to *work fast*. Prowling rural towns like Hoffman and the areas surrounding them like wolves on the hunt, they searched for any easy way they could find to make a jump up in life. They were men on the make, and Colonel George Jackson Caine was smack dab in the big middle of them.

— 7 —

BEWARE OF BONNIE TIGER!

UPON GLANCING TO THE WEST as they rode their horses at a slow walk down the east side of Main Street, the main north-west street of their community, after a morning of hunting down in the Deep Fork River bottom, Nolen Sessions asked his cousin Warren, "Who's that goin' into Harmony's Store? I don't remember ever seein' her before, but she doesn't look half bad to me. She's kind of cute, in fact. What do you say we ease over that way and say hello as we go by? Nothin' ventured, nothin' gained," he grinned, "so why don't we give it a go? Who knows, we might hit it off!"

It was not surprising that Nolen hadn't seen the girl before, since he and his family had only recently arrived in the growing farm community. His father had settled there for the same reason as Warren's father and most everybody else: to capitalize on the low-priced land that had become available in the area, which until only recently had been the exclusive domain of the Creek Indian citizens of the Oklahoma Indian Territory. Warren and Nolen's fathers were brothers, and they were ambitious men who were more than willing to work hard to get ahead. Both families were from the same town in Missouri.

Warren's family made their move three years earlier; Nolen's family had recently joined them.

The cousins' fathers had the same goal in life, which was to earn enough through their own hard labor to pay off mortgages they had taken out to buy the plots of land they were farming. Their intention was to become debt-free landowners so they could be independent and live on their own terms. They had a long way to go, but both men took for granted that that they were on an upward track.

"Yeah," Warren answered Nolen. "I know exactly who she is, and your problem is that you don't have any idea what you're lookin' at. You're only seein' the package, not the girl up close. Her name is Bonnie Tiger, but nobody calls her that. Everybody calls her Tiger. Tiger is a well-known and well-respected Creek family surname out here, but the same can't be said for her immediate family. Her mother's already dead and gone, so now there's only her and her father. To a person, everyone I've talked to has recommended that I stay as far away from the Tigers as possible. They're bad news, is what I've been told.

Her old man's name is Early Tiger. You saw the guy who went into the store a minute before her, the big guy; that was him. He's nothin' but a local drunk, and he's one of the big-deal, fallin' down, all-the-way-gone types, too. You'll start seein' him here and there around town after you've been here for a while, and, when you do, he'll be as drunk as a skunk. He stays that way, they say, whenever he can, and he's in and out of jail for drunkenness or theft as regular as clockwork.

Everybody says the girl's as crazy as hell," Warren continued. "She's her old man's caretaker, whenever he's not locked up and living at home. People say he'd steal the feathers off a chicken, just to show it can be done. I've been told that he wanders off whenever he takes a notion, leaving her alone out where they live. They live together in an old shack he has out on the outskirts of town. I'm as interested in women as you are," he said, "but both of us can do a hell of a lot better that that one.

If you're seriously interested, you'd better take a good look at her while you can, since you'll rarely ever see her around. They live like a couple of hermits. You see them together only when they come in to pick up mail and buy necessities. Even then, he usually comes in alone. You'll see him a lot more often than you do her, but only because he comes in by himself again and again, always lookin' to get drunk and slink around in search of anything he can get his hands on to steal. He's a constant pain in the butt. Just ask Sheriff Cox about him: He'll give you an earful you won't soon forget.

Beyond what I've told you, that father and daughter pair are like a couple of ghosts. For Christ's sake," Warren said in summary, "if you lived like recluses the way those two do, you'd be messed up and crazy too.   My advice, on the outside chance that you do somehow happen to wrangle a way to get up close to her and end up getting' what you're after, is that you'll be smart to beware of Bonnie Tiger. Like I said, everybody I've talked to says she and her father are bad news!"

Nolen, after pondering the advice he'd been given, decided that the wisest course of action would be to heed what his cousin had to say.   Why, he figured, should he waste any effort trying to get something going with a girl who was known to have as many problems as her?   In their area, unattached females weren't as available as apples dangling from trees, but he knew that Warren had made an excellent point.   Even in their isolated location, they did have better options.   So, after no more than the few words that had passed between the cousins, two more eligible young men did what a whole string of others had done before them: They rode on past Tiger, in search of less complicated pickings.

In the same way as cousins Nolen and Warren Sessions, four budding matrons—Coraleen Townsend, Viva Swinney, Oleta Rhodes, and Velva Nix— also watched that day as Early and his daughter Tiger walked out of Harmony's Store and boarded their wagon.   The ladies saw them from the south on the west side of Main Street, in their case as they talked with one another outside the post office. They were good friends, mothers whose habit it was to meet once a week at a prearranged hour to pick up mail and do their grocery shopping.

With their mail in hand, the four ladies hurried from the post office to Harmony's Store, where they sat down at a table and set of chairs that were situated next to a wall-mounted bulletin board. The board was mounted on a wall beside a potbellied stove on which Mr. Harmony brewed a big pot of coffee every morning. Their weekly meetings were a welcome opportunity to get away from their husbands and kids for a while, have a cup of coffee, flip through their mail, talk about the assorted items that were posted for sale on the bulletin board, and, most important of all, to chatter with one another like a flock of hens.

Gossip spread like a house afire once they got rolling, and the greater part of what they talked about on this date had to do with Tiger and her father. Because Early Tiger and his daughter Bonnie were reclusive people, they weren't seen together all that often. When they were, it was news—mini-news, of course, but still news, and each one of the ladies had something to say about what they had just seen.

"Did you get a good look at the clothes that poor girl was wearing?" Coraleen exclaimed to Viva, Oleta, and Velva. "They looked like she'd been sleeping in them for a week. You'd think even she would have more pride than to come into town looking like that. She's plenty old enough to wash her and her father's clothes, for crying out loud.   She ought to have more pride than that, shouldn't she, no matter what she's been through."

As the four of them nodded their heads in agreement, Oleta asked if the other three had taken a good look at Tiger's hair?   "What a tangled mess it was," she said.   "I'd be willing to bet she hasn't combed it in a month.   No matter how little they have or how poorly they live out at their place, a woman ought to be proud enough to comb her hair before she leaves her house.   There's no excuse for not taking basic care of yourself.   You don't need a mother, a set of instructions, or a lot of money to know that you need to do that."   Once again, all four heads nodded in agreement.

Their discussion went on in this same vein for a while, until Viva summarized matters with respect to Early Tiger and Bonnie for all four of them by declaring, "What in the world is going to become of that girl? She can't stay out there forever, living with her father.   Who's she going to marry?   What man with any sense won't figure out that he ought not to take up with her as she is?   If she doesn't get herself together, she's going to end up an old maid for the rest of her life.   She's already pretty far along in that direction, it seems to me."

The portion of the ladies' gossip session that had to do with Early Tiger's family didn't come to an end until Velva, as one of them inevitably did, offered up a new version of the same admonition that always summed up their collective assessment of his daughter's dilemma, which was that that anyone who had any sense—or more to the point, any *single* man—most definitely ought to beware of Bonnie Tiger. The girl, all four ladies agreed, was far too troubled to be a good match for any halfway decent beau. Once their jointly held sentiment was restated for the record, discussion of the Tiger family ended, and the focus of their attention shifted to an entirely different topic. The rest of their time together that day was devoted to intense evaluation of the items other neighbors had posted for sale on Mr. Harmony's bulletin board.

Interactions of the kind that took place between the four matrons and cousins Nolen and Warren Sessions illustrated how Tiger and her father were held in extremely low esteem by neighbors and other residents of their hometown. Having a bad reputation was tragic enough for Tiger in and of itself, but what made things even harder for her was that her status stemmed far more from having been born into an abysmal domestic homelife than to anything she said or did herself. It was unfair of people to look down on her as they did, but they did it anyhow, and they did it with impunity. Knowing how others talked about her made Tiger's life miserable, but there wasn't a single thing she could do about it.

By the time she reached young adulthood, everyone in the community was aware of her troubles and knew she was warped to an extent seldom seen in someone of her age and gender. It hurt her to the quick when she overheard in bits and snatches what people had to say about herself and her family. Considering how negatively she and her father were talked about, no fair-minded person should blame her for having wished a pox on every one of her neighbors.

Bonnie's personal and familial problems were more than public knowledge; they were matters of intense local scrutiny as well. Her mother's story was revelatory and salacious enough to have been condensed into a regional cautionary tale that was referred to as "The Story of Mock's Bad Stomp," and her father Early's antics and escapades were so well known that they had been the subject of local gossip for as long as she could remember. Because her own poor reputation had initially been acquired more through association with her parents' nefarious activities rather than antics of her own, it could be said that she came by it honestly.

Her problem worsened, however, as she grew older, after she started acting out in frustration. As she was growing up, it began to seem that every step she took was calculated to tarnish a reputation that was bad enough already.

Her childhood and young adult years could have been worse for Tiger, but it is difficult to imagine how.   Sensible people don't speak of life as being *fair* or *unfair*, but there most definitely are instances when it appears to take on an exceptional cruelty. Tiger's young life is definitive proof of that.   During her tenderest years she was subjected to unforgivably harsh mistreatment and neglect at the hands of her own parents, and it had the predictably awful effects that result from that kind of abuse.

Bonnie's girlhood years were an absolute nightmare, and that interlude of extreme vulnerability was followed by teenage years during which her already dreadful conditions got even worse.   It is only natural to wonder how she got caught up in in such an outrageously terrible predicament, and, of course, to wonder what became of her in the end.   For answers to these questions and to be able to understand later events, it is necessary to summarize her childhood story, as tragic as it was.

— 8 —

HOW BONNIE
BECAME TIGER

BONNIE TIGER WAS BORN on January 15, 1883, to Early and Etta Jane "Mock" (Burnham) Tiger out in the Creek Nation of the Indian Territory of pre-statehood Oklahoma, where they lived in an out-of-the-way settlement so obscure it was referred to on maps as a *populated place* rather than a named location. Partly as a play on their family surname but mostly because the girl was so often sick, whiny, and fretful as she was growing up, Etta chose *Tiger* as a pet name for her daughter. Picking up on her mother's practice, it didn't take long for neighbors, family members, and the rest of the community to begin referring to her as Tiger as well. Because it fit so well, the nickname took hold. Within a few years, it became *her*, so to speak, as if she had never had another first name. She became Tiger to everyone, and, from that point forward, that's what she was called.

The greatest misfortune of Tiger's life was an accident of birth. She was born into a family built around a highly dysfunctional marital relationship, a union toxic enough to create developmental damage that lasted for the rest of her life. Throughout her girlhood years, she had no choice but to contend with circumstances that would have been harmful to any child.

Her parents were not merely unhappy in marriage; they literally hated their marital relationship, as well as one another. In addition, they resented having to raise a child, especially a child that neither one of them made any pretense of loving. Tiger had to live with the curse of her own parents' unapologetically indifferent attitudes toward her, on top of the normal growing pains every youngster has deal with as they move forward in life. Growing up in such smothering surroundings would have been difficult for any child to bear, but, for Tiger, due to how sickly and behaviorally troubled she was, it was an all-consuming challenge.

Because she was no more than a hapless kid, Tiger was unable to comprehend why her parents were so remote and uncaring toward her, nor could she understand why they treated her as badly as they did, but, even if she had been able to understand them, it would have made no difference; their neglect would have persisted either way. For a child, there's no way out of a predicament like hers, no matter how difficult or unfair it may be. Their only choice is to shut up and do what they're told, whether they like it or not, and that, of course, was what Tiger had to do.

Tiger's mother Etta was a distant, unaffectionate, indifferent parent, a mother who had no natural interest in nurturing or caregiving. She did no more than she had to, just to get Tiger through her childhood years. She paid minimal attention to how clean she was, nor did she comb her hair or help her dress. The consequence of her neglect was that Tiger always looked like a rag mop. She was poorly clothed, fed carelessly, and treated more like an unwanted pet than as an innocent child. Neighbors who knew what was going on wondered how the poor kid made it through her younger years. To their surprise, though, she did.

Although it was clear to neighbors that her parents' miserable relationship was the core cause of Tiger's miserable upbringing, their general knowledge of what she had to contend with didn't prove to be of any practical help as she grew older. Even if one of them had wanted to intervene, there wasn't much of anything they could have done to improve her circumstances. In their corner of the world, it would have been considered meddling for anyone to try to tell a married couple how to run their household or raise their children. Unless internal matters spilled over in a way as to have an adverse effect on the larger community, such a thing was never done. Typically, people tended to mind their own business and leave others alone to mind theirs.

Everyone who knew the Early Tiger family—and, in their community, everybody knew everybody—was aware of the appalling circumstances in which Tiger was being raised. It was known, for example, that the girl had no choice but to grow up watching and listening to her parents' ever-escalating arguments and fights. In their setting, one couple's incessant battling usually ended up common knowledge, especially when it was impossible to avoid. As painful as it was for father, mother, and daughter alike, argumentation between her parents never let up.

The primary cause of Tiger and her mother's misery was Early's alcoholism. It was a curse that hung over their household like a dark cloud, an affliction that first magnified his many grievances and then turned him into an indignant, frustrated man. Unhappy with his lot in life, he was one of those men who didn't hesitate to take out his frustration on his own wife and child. His abuse was as regular as it was severe.

He complained bitterly to anyone who would listen about how he was unable to provide decent food and suitable clothing for his family, but he always found a way to buy all the cigarettes and alcohol he wanted. He smoked like a chimney and stayed drunk all the time, while his wife and child were left to do without. For Early Tiger, his incessant drunkenness was an absolute scourge, a disease that tormented him as much as it did everyone around him—who, in the end, amounted to his wife Etta, who was called Mock, and, of course, Tiger.

Uninhibited by any effective social mechanisms to keep him from doing so, Early felt free to "correct" his wife in any way he felt necessary, and, as their years together rolled by, he made a regular practice of doing exactly that, with little inhibition or restraint. Because it was considered highly intrusive and bad form for anyone to try to interfere with what went on inside a private home, neighbors never questioned his authority as a husband to discipline his wife. As there were few restrictions on what he could get away with, Early evolved into an in-your-face bully as well as an uncaring brute, both combined in the same package. Whenever Etta did not obey any aspect of what he considered to be his legitimate husbandly demands, he would, in his own words, proceed to "teach her pretty good."

A woman's personal and social prerogatives at the time were nothing like they are today, especially in a backwater Indian community like theirs. Etta (or Mock) didn't think there was anything that could be done about the way Early treated her, not by her or by anyone else. Resigned to her fate, she was unable to envision any alternative but to stay fixed where she was, putting up with whatever treatment Early meted out.

Because she had had to get married, Etta believed that she deserved any fate that was dealt out to her. Others had convinced her that she was where she was solely due to her own failings, so she thought she had no choice but to make the best of whatever came her way. She was resigned to doing so, no matter how dreadful her situation became. She knew there was no one she could call on for help if conditions got too far out of hand, because she had estranged herself from those who ordinarily would have been her defenders. That, too, she believed in heart and mind, was nobody's fault but her own.

Based on this sort of reasoning, Tiger's mother Mock acquiesced to and accepted the authority of her husband to treat her as badly as he did, conceiving of her awful treatment as being "what she deserved" and as "just how it was." Seeing her predicament in that light had the unintended effect of making it even easier for Early to demean her with impunity.

As the years slowly ground by, Tiger's mother continued to confront her fate stoically, effectively empowering her father to take for granted that it was his prerogative to treat her as brutally and as indifferently as he liked. He terrorized and battered her for as long as they were together, from their first day as a couple until the last. Their relationship started out on a bad note, and it ended on a worse note, as if they had become tone deaf.

Their pitiful marriage was as miserable for Tiger as it was for her parents, since she had no choice but to watch in tearful silence as her father forcefully abused her mother. Watching her mother being battered was a common occurrence in their home, something as ordinary as getting up in the morning. Whether her father was drunk or sober, there was no way to tell what might set him off, and it never took much to do so. He had a violent temper, and he was always worse when he came home drunk. It got so bad that Tiger began to think of battering as a normal part of a marital relationship.

During her tender childhood years, fear of her father's violence became a fact of everyday life. All Tiger could do was try to stay out of his way, getting by as best she could. That's about all kids who live with drunken bullies can do. Throughout her younger years, this was how things stayed.

*****

Just when Tiger had begun to think that conditions in their home couldn't get any worse, they did precisely that. The exact date it happened is unknown, but, one day in July of 1891, Tiger's mother Mock's years of extreme abuse came to an abrupt and unexpected end when she disappeared from the residence she had shared with her husband and daughter for over eight years. It happened totally out of the blue, without an explanation of any kind. One moment she was there, and the next moment she was not; and, once she was gone, she was gone for good. From that point forward, not a single word from her or about her was ever heard.

No one in the community had any idea what had become of Etta. Their neighbors knew only that Mock had been living an awful life with an alcoholic husband who had made it known that he hated her. These clear-cut realities at once caused most everyone to conclude that he surely had to be responsible for her disappearance. Early was everyone's suspect number one from the very beginning.

Unsurprisingly, their neighbors put forward all kinds of theories about why Tiger's mother so suddenly disappeared from the face of the earth. Under the circumstances, speculation about what may or may not have happened to her had to be expected. A half dozen or more rational explanations for Mock's disappearance were seriously considered, but only those accounts that in one way or another involved her husband seemed plausible. For this reason, most eyes remained focused on Early.

Early's straightforward explanation for his wife's absence was to bluntly assert that she had "run off and left him with a daughter to care for, probably for another man. Oh, she'll come back," he predicted, "just as soon as the ungrateful bitch gets cold and hungry." Beyond that, he didn't have anything more to say. "She's the one who run off," he complained, "so why in the hell are all of you trying to make me feel guilty about it, when I didn't do a damned thing!"

Early's assertions were doubted from the get-go, mainly because people considered Tiger's mother Mock too browbeaten, mousy, terrorized, and backward to have mustered up enough courage to do anything that justifiably bold. At the same time, though, they knew running away was exactly what they would have done themselves, if they had been saddled with circumstances as outrageous as hers.

Unending speculation took place thereafter over what may or may not have happened to Mock, but, in the end, neither husband nor daughter nor anyone else ever officially reported Etta "Mock" (Burnham) Tiger missing. Sheriff Cox had heard all about her disappearance, but her absence wasn't a crime and there was no overt evidence of anything criminal having happened.

Tiger was one of those who had no difficulty believing that she had run away by choice, due to her up-close-and-personal knowledge of the horrible abuse her mother had had put with over the years. She accepted as gospel truth her father's assertion that Mock had abandoned them, probably because she, too, like so many others, thought it would have been a sensible path for her mother to have taken. More likely than not, Tiger secretly wished she had been bold enough to do the same thing. In any case, Tiger didn't even consider questioning her father's version of events; even if she had had doubts, living in abject fear of what he might do if she disagreed with him in any way would have silenced them.

In the end, it was not possible to say with any degree of certainty what had become of Tiger's mother. It was easy to believe that she might have deserted her family, just as Early had asserted. That possibility certainly did not seem at all far-fetched, given the miserable life she had been living under her husband's roof. Because she had never been any more than marginally close to her mother, Tiger knew that concern for her personal welfare wouldn't have been enough to keep her mother at home.

Normally, the disappearance of a young woman, especially a mother, would have been a matter of highest concern within a community, but the plain truth in Mock's case was that her absence did not elicit any appreciable level of formal discussion, let alone a detailed investigation. Early's comments seemed to have been accepted at face value. It really didn't seem unreasonable to think that she might have taken off on her own, probably as a conse-quence of yet another domestic blowout within their household. Over the years, one crazy thing after an-other, people reasoned, had happened out at their miserable excuse for a home. If Tiger's mother had snuck off in search of a new start, then hooray for her, people seemed to have thought, knowing that that's what they would have done, if they had been in her shoes.

During the months and years after her mother's disappearance, not a single serious advocate or protector ever came forward to speak on her behalf. Her own parents passed before she disappeared, but, even if they hadn't, they wouldn't have spoken up for her either, since they had disowned her years before. Other members of her extended family had done the same. Due to the well-deserved nefarious reputations she and her husband had built up, no one wanted to get involved in any aspect of their affairs. They had heard enough about Mock and Early to last them for a lifetime.

When the subject of her mother's absence came up during the years that followed, it was raised more as a matter of casual speculation than as a topic worthy of substantial discussion or serious investigation. There was no evidence for anyone to investigate, anyway.

Did Tiger's father Early do away with her mother, as most people had suspected? Could he have flown into a rage, beaten her to death, and buried her somewhere out in the woods? Sure, that was possible, but it was equally possible that, as he claimed, nothing untoward had happened to her at all. She might have left on her own accord, just as he said. No dead body had ever turned up in the vicinity, which meant that any one eventuality was as just plausible as any other. Even so, it would have come as no surprise to anyone to learn that the worst that could have happened had, in fact, happened.

What it all came down to in the end was that no one ever considered it their responsibility or made a mission of doing any real investigation of what happened to Mock. More likely than not, nothing would have come of it, even if they had. She was just gone. Nothing was heard from her after her disappearance, and that's how the matter was left to stand. Eventually, people dropped the subject and stopped talking about it.

Unfortunately for Tiger, her mother's disappearance truly was yet another terrible blow for her, but not due to the sadness that normally goes with the loss of a parent. The real blow to Tiger was that her mother had been her only foil against her father, and even marginal protection from his rages had been better than no defense at all. With her mother gone, her fear was that the mistreatment she had experienced up to that point in life would become worse than ever, and, sadly, that was exactly what happened.

*****

From the age of eight and up through the rest of her youthful years, Early Tiger became Tiger's only parent, and, in that role, he made no effort at all to be dutiful toward her. Having rejected her as being his legitimate daughter, he paid no real attention at all to her welfare. Tiger had no choice but to get by on her own, doing the best she could, using whatever she could find to work with.

She got by, but only by living on the lousiest of food, dressing in the raggediest of clothing, and fending for herself, all due to having been rejected by and then ignored by her father Early. Saying only that she was *neglected* amounts to understating how badly she was treated during her years of highest vulnerability, because it implies that she dealt with only garden variety indifference when her home conditions were far worse than that.

Her father kept her out of school as often as he could, made her feed and care for herself, and, as young as she was, didn't hesitate for a moment to use her as a personal servant whenever he was at home, terrorizing her all the while. He paid attention to her only when he needed something, or when she behaved in some way that he considered inappropriate.

Early earned a living by growing and selling a few crops, keeping up a home garden, and, on occasion, from raising and selling a horse, cow, or hog. For more income, he trained horses that were boarded at his place and did piecework and other odd jobs as openings of that kind became available. In addition, he hunted for game and caught fish out of creeks and ponds and the nearby Deep Fork River bottom. He topped off these sources of income by stealing anything he could get his hands on without getting caught. He brought in enough to get by on as well as to buy all the smokes he wanted and enough alcohol to stay drunk most of the time, but he hardly spent a dime on keeping up a decent home for his daughter.

Whenever he left home for one of his bouts of drunken carousing, he would leave instructions for Tiger. "Slop the hogs, milk the cows, throw out grain for the chickens, and keep the garden weeded," he would say, warning that he would check on things when he got back. Tiger learned the hard way that she'd get a whipping if she did not do what she was told.

Tiger had grown used to being neglected, to living with rejection, and to being treated like a rag mop, even before her mother's disappearance. Being left alone with her father only upped the ante. The main difference between her parenting behavior and his was that he thought nothing of terrifying her into absolute obedience, while her mother had been more verbally than physically abusive.

As Tiger grew into her teenage years, it would have come as no surprise to anyone to learn that her father began to "train" his daughter in the same way he had trained her mother before her. As far as he was concerned, his approach had worked well with Mock—at least, that is, until she, as he told anyone who asked about her, ran off with another man, which, from his perspective, was no nobody's fault but her own. He handled his women in his way and in his way alone, no matter how badly things turned out at home.

In their day and setting, parents considered sparing the rod to be a sure way of spoiling a child, and her father wholeheartedly subscribed to this convenient philosophy. Conceptualizing his parental responsibility in those terms not only affirmed his own natural inclinations but also supplied the few added degrees of license needed for him to feel free to discipline Tiger in the most deliberate and calculated of ways.

He resented having been pushed into marrying Tiger's mother because she was pregnant, and he resented even more that he had unexpectedly ended up with sole responsibility for having to raise a child, especially a child he continued to insist might not even be his own. He thought of his daughter in the same way he thought of her mother before her—that she was a person with low moral standards, one more female who would most certainly be susceptible to the rampant promiscuity in the world around and about them. It was for these reasons that his behavior toward Tiger was in every way as harsh, irrational, and unfair as it sounds upon explanation.

He was determined to steer Tiger away from any manner of reckless behavior, and it was his goal to do so well before it was too late for meaningful intervention. To make sure Tiger adhered to the high standards he demanded, he punished any real or imaginary infraction she committed, often on no more than a whim. He routinely subjected her to punishment so severe that she was terrified to death of him for the rest of their years together. Tiger was even more cowed by his presence than her mother had been before her.

Whenever Tiger strayed over one of her father's arbitrarily drawn behavioral lines, she paid a steep price. Browbeating, slapping, whipping with a belt, denial of necessities, and other imaginative forms of punishment became a normal part of her daily existence. Kids have lived in households so miserable as to be unimaginable to those who are fortunate enough to enjoy a normal upbringing, and Tiger most definitely was one of them. There were neighbors who knew how badly her father was treating her, but not a one of them ever said a word about it.

It has often been asked over the years if Tiger had been sexually as well as corporeally and psychologically abused, but that question was never conclusively answered. If she was mistreated in that way, she never spoke of it, nor, as would be expected, did her father.   Those who carefully considered this possibility usually concluded that that sort of abuse had not been one of her problems, mainly because her father treated her so badly that they were emotionally and personally distant from one another.   Little investigation was needed to learn that she had been nothing more than his domestic servant and that he had hated her as much as she hated him.   Even though it seemed unlikely, the possibility of his having taken sexual advantage of her remained an ever-present topic of speculation.

*****

"It is absolutely correct to think it was the way her father treated her," some of their neighbors were said to have claimed years after the Tiger family's drama was over and done with, "that caused the girl to grow up to be the promiscuous, grasping, manipulative, social-climbing schemer she became later in life.   What else," they'd sigh, "could have been expected?"

Comments along these lines were nothing more than self-exonerating hindsight, but they were made on occasion by neighbors who, after it was way too late to matter, felt guilty about what had happened to Tiger, right under their noses.   Outcomes are always clear after the fact.   The truth of the matter was that not even one of them ever intervened on her behalf, back when an outside comment might have been helpful.

Those who were quickest to ridicule or criticize how Tiger behaved during her struggle toward adulthood tended to be the same ones who never tried to lift her spirits or help her out in any way. If she had not helped herself during her younger years, she would have had no help at all. She got by, but it was a miracle she did.

It should be no wonder to anyone that Tiger grew up to become a maladjusted and unusual young woman, since she had had to get by without any real nurturing and through surviving on the scantest of essentials. Her drunken, surly father provided only sporadic care, and even that had been grudgingly given. Just as her father had all along, she grew up subsisting on home garden produce, fish caught out of local creeks and ponds, any game that could be shot or trapped, nuts, berries, greens harvested off slag mounds at the sites of long-defunct mines, and occasional government handouts of food and clothing. To earn spending money, she did occasional odd jobs for neighbors, just like her father had before her. She got along by hook or by crook, doing whatever had to be done to get by from one day to the next.

It was not readily discernible from looking at her that Tiger was a severely wounded person, but that is exactly what she was. Psychological damage isn't always visible, but it can be as painful as any bodily wound. Her problems were manifested in the form of behaviors, values, and attitudes that neither she nor anyone else ever rightly understood. Having been raised in a miserable home situation like hers, it should come as no surprise to anyone that she grew up to be a conspicuously insecure and unbalanced young woman.

Tiger wasn't held in high esteem by the peers and neighbors of her teenaged years, and that's describing her social status as benignly as possible. She compounded her problems by being exceptionally difficult to deal with as a young person, until she built up a record for being irresponsible as well as for having a terribly negative attitude. She had trouble getting along with everyone.

Tiger grew up living the same way as her father—on the fringes of society, emotionally isolated, and existing in her own private world. It was so widely believed that things would eventually go badly for her that all conjecture about her future had less to do with *if* thing were going to go bad and much more with *how* and *when* the axe would finally fall.

*****

It was through overhearing bits and snatches of information during her late childhood and early teenage years that Tiger became aware of the deeds and misdeeds of her own parents. In isolated towns, people never forget, especially once they learn something spicy about someone else, something that can be brought up to make them feel superior. Her parents' negative reputations made them frequent subjects of local gossip, no matter how much Tiger hated hearing others going on about them. To her, it never stopped.

It didn't take long for her to realize that every Tom, Dick, and Harry in Hoffman and the surrounding area knew all kinds of dirt about her folks, and not just due to ordinary small-town gossip. Their misdeeds had been instructive enough for a full-fledged cautionary tale to have begun circulating about them. Referred to as "The Story of Mock's Bad Stomp," it was an excruciatingly detailed and painfully graphic account of her own parents' young lives. Everybody in the area seemed to know all about them.

According to the story, her mother's disobedience had been the root cause of every misfortune that befell her, including how and why she ended up having to marry her father Early. Her mother was already gone, back when all of this was getting off the ground. Had she been around to defend herself, she might have been able to stave off being cast in such a negative light.

Another depressingly painful family fact that was disclosed in "Mock's Bad Stomp" had to do with how Tiger's mother had abandoned her husband and a young daughter only eight years old to run off with an unknown man. The source of this information, she knew from having been there when it happened, was her father Early, whose explanation of her disappearance seemed to have been accepted as gospel truth, even though there had been no way to prove his assertions. Unfortunately, there had been no way to disprove them, either. But, whether his version of events was true or not, Tiger knew for sure that he had been left with the responsibility for caring for a daughter, because that daughter was her.

No young woman growing up could have felt good about herself or about her family after hearing a batch of tales like those that were revealed in "Mock's Bad Stomp." To Tiger, local bantering about her parents seemed to go on forever. To her way of thinking, their story was an absolute curse, an out-and-out torment. Whenever she overheard people talking about it, she felt like dirt beneath their feet. Under her breath, she cursed every person who made disparaging comments about her parents, but that was all she was able to do. She had to listen, whether she wanted to or not.

One of her greatest wishes growing up was that every personal family matter could have been kept totally out of the public eye. In her case, though, that had been impossible. Any chance she might have had to enjoy any privacy was long gone, thanks to the nefarious activities of her own parents and the rampant gossip that went on about them. From the day she was born, her life was an open book, no matter how fervently she wished things had been otherwise.

Tiger ended up being a young woman who was only partially socialized, someone who was *different*, but not in clear ways. Most of her problems were invisible to the naked eye, but she most definitely had them—a lot of them. As she was growing older, she looked much like any other young woman, aside from usually being unkempt and tackily dressed. She wasn't normal, though, not in the least.

Tiger was set apart by mannerisms, values, attitudes, and quirks that were anything but ordinary, on top of having next to no social skills or impulse control to speak of. She was not sufficiently acculturated to know how to behave around people, which meant that she was unable to understand how her behavior came across to others.

She had a fearsome-sounding nickname, but Tiger was anything but a strong and discerning young person. When it came to the management of her own personal affairs, the truth of the matter was that she was a person who hung on by the slenderest of threads. Due to her well known problems, she was considered something of a pariah in the little pond that was her hometown.

— 9 —

GROWING UP
DURING TROUBLING
TIMES

BECAUSE BONNIE TIGER WAS RAISED in extreme poverty as she inched her way toward maturity, there always was a full plate of woe on her table. On top of her miserable home circumstances and many behavioral difficulties, she, like most other Indian residents of the territory, also had to deal with the uncertainties of the early 1900s, of which there were many. For her, growing up was anything but the easy and carefree phase of life that it is for most young people.

Although she was about as politically unaware and socially uninvolved as it was possible for a young person to be, the years between her birth in 1883 and the date on which she turned 21 in 1904 was a time of such tumultuous change in her region of the country that there was no way she could avoid the spinoff effects of what was going on. The goings-on were perturbing, not just for her but for the entirety of the Creek tribe as well as for most other Indian residents of the area.

For various reasons, the tribes of the territory had been in a shaky position for many years, but their primary problem stemmed from the blunt forces that were being exerted by powerful outsiders who coveted the land upon which they lived. Pressure from these forces had become an inescapable fact of life for all Indian people, and it left them feeling threatened and uncertain and, therefore, insecure.

Complicating this intractable problem for the Tigers and most other Indian people of the territory was that their troubles were not well understood—or, for that matter, particularly cared about—by those who wielded political power during these worrying years. Understanding the dynamics that were at play goes a long way in terms of explaining why her father Early and then later Tiger herself preferred self-imposed isolation over more contact with territorial outsiders. There were good reasons why many of their peers felt this way.

Like her father and mother before her, Tiger was born a resident of the Creek Nation of the Oklahoma Indian Territory during years when the independent social structure their people had lived under for as long as they could remember was going through a period of dramatic change. The Creek Nation was an isolated place until the late 1800s, with its citizens living in a location most whites didn't know much about. This began to change in a big way in the years prior to Oklahoma's becoming a state of the union. Tiger and her father were caught up in several key events that forever changed their lives and the lives of their Indian neighbors.

The Creeks, after having been forcibly "removed" and "resettled" from their original homelands in the eastern part of the United States to their new tribal location in the Oklahoma Territory, had ended up on land that white as well as black settlers and developers, along with other powerful interest groups, wanted for themselves It mattered only minimally to these groups that the land they coveted had been assigned to the tribe by the federal government; they were intent on pushing farther onto Indian Territory at every opportunity.

These outside groups didn't care much about the treaties and boundary rights that existed at that point, and they ignored them whenever they could get away with it. Their intrusion was trespassing, but it happened anyway. Cattle raisers, railroad companies, illegal settlers, and others exerted steady pressure on the federal government to open for white settlement any land that was not specifically assigned (as well as some that was) for Indian homesteads, communities, and developments.

The formerly independent and self-governing Creeks weren't strong enough or politically astute enough to escape the clutches of the scheming parties that were eager to lay hands on their land, interests that never stopped conniving and devising legal or quasi-legal mechanisms designed to separate them from what was rightfully theirs. The Creeks were only one of many tribes that were plagued by this problem.

Due to various complicating factors, the federal government did not (and some say did not want to) protect the Indians or the land that had been set aside for them. Indian leaders realized what the intrusion of more white settlers would mean to their race and to ownership of their land, but they lacked the political force required to change the course of events. Numerous boundary and jurisdictional changes continued to sweep through Oklahoma over the years, and all of them had the effect of pushing the Indians into an ever-decreasing amount of space.

The excuse the federal government needed to finally strip the Creek Indians of their last jointly owned land was provided by the Civil War. What happened during the war was that many of the Creeks, like most (but not all) of the other Indian tribes in the territory, chose to side with the South rather than the Union. They sided with the Confederacy due to its hostility to their common enemy, the federal government, and due to southern leaders' belief in the concept of state rights and regional autonomy. If the Southerners were to win the war, the Creeks figured, they would be much more likely to sympathize with the Indians' desire for independence than the Union, which was dominated by northern and eastern whites who believed in a strong and centralized federal government.

The Creeks, like some other tribes, were already at internal odds with one another when this fateful decision was made. Most of the Indians had no use for whites of any political persuasion, but some of their main leaders thought the South had only the slimmest chance of winning and that siding with them, therefore, would end in disaster for their people. What came about was a self-destructive internal split, one that led to one faction of the Creeks fighting for the South and another faction fighting for the North. Creek soldiers on each side fought fierce and bloody battles against one another during the war. That this was happening had to have been confusing and trying for every member of the tribe, regardless of their personal political predilections.

When the South was defeated in 1865, the federal government had all the justification that was needed to, in effect, punish the Indians for siding against the Union. Retribution came in the form of insisting that the resettled tribes renegotiate their land treaties as compensation. The major motivation for renegotiating the treaties all along was that doing so would clear the way to opening more land for white settlement and, with the same stroke of the pen, make room for freed black slaves, people the government had promised to help after the end of the war.

The treaty renegotiations that followed effectively dismantled not only the concept of Indian self-government but also did away with a large part of the tribal ownership of land and the reservation system as well. The overall amount of land set aside for reservations was vastly reduced by the new treaties, even as more Indian tribes from other parts of the country were re-settled in the Indian Territory during the years that followed.

What all of this meant on a practical level for Indians who lived in the territory was that they were eventually rendered even more vulnerable to exploitation by sophisticated white speculators, developers, and settlers than they already were. Before the era was over, a good number of them ended up losing their shirts due to changes that were forced upon the tribes.

The specific legal framework that was employed by Congress to free up more Indian Territory land for settlement was the Dawes Act of 1887. The act was designed to deal with the special needs of Indians that had been confined to reservations, but the effect of it was to bring an end to traditional tribal life and push the Indians into adopting white modes of living. The tribes themselves were dissolved under the act, and tribal ownership of lands was ended.

Individual land ownership, a concept that was still unfamiliar and suspect among many Indians and therefore not supported by them, became the law of the land. Each married Indian male was allotted 160 acres to farm, and each adult single man or woman received 80 acres. Freed blacks were conveniently designated "adoptees" of the various tribes, thereby creating a legal justification for giving them allotment land as well. This gave the federal government a way of living up to promises made to black freedmen who supported the Union during the war.

After the Indian tribal land was broken into identifiable parcels and deeded over to individual Indian and Freedman allottees, the new landowners eventually (but not at once) became free to sell or transfer their land rights as they wished. Concurrently, the Dawes Act also made it possible for outsiders to claim and settle on any land that was not specifically allotted to individual Indians or blacks. This action opened large tracts of the Indian Territory for white settlement. Predictably, white investors, speculators, and settlers, who recognized a good oppor-tunity when they saw one, flocked to these areas to take as much advantage of them as they could.

There is a record to show that a great loss of Indian land occurred while all these changes were happening, and hard figures are available as confirmation. In 1873, at the beginning of the reservation policy, the Indian reservations had about 150 million acres; in 1887, when the Dawes Act was passed, the amount dropped to 138 million. By 1900, the "Oklahoma Territory" had been expanded to encompass the entire western half of the present-day State of Oklahoma and even more, while the "Indian Territory" had been reduced to the eastern section.

On a practical level, what all these changes meant is that in a few short years, millions of acres of land that had been in the hands of the Indians ended up in the hands of whites or blacks. Due to the environment of uncertainty and confusion that prevailed, most tribal people didn't realize the impact these changes would have on them over the long haul. The Tigers, for example, were among those who had no clue what it would mean to them.

— 10 —

THE BIRTH OF HOFFMAN TOWNSITE

EARLY TIGER AND HIS DAUGHTER Bonnie were among the thousands of Indians who lived in one of those sections of the territory that had become attractive to outsiders. Developers, speculators, businessmen, and ordinary folks in search of low-cost land on which to start a ranch or a farm could hardly wait to get their hands on it, and aggressive pursuit of any and every possibility for doing so was the order of the day.   Getting a toehold on Indian land was thought to be a great way for an enterprising person to get ahead in life, and a good many people were willing to go to great lengths to make sure that's how it turned out for them.

Whenever the federal government opened any new Indian land for settlement, outsiders flocked to the area in swaths, all of them looking to claim a personal piece of the pie in one way or another.   The tactics some of these aggressive outsiders used perplexed and threatened the Indian people of the Territory.

The Tiger family's geographical area was considered promising by many hopeful newcomers because it was fertile and full of game and natural resources. Due to a high annual rainfall, it was an area that stayed green for most of the year, which meant that plenty of grass was available for grazing horses and cattle.   In addition, there were large groves of valuable hardwood timber—oak, hickory, black walnut, and pecan—in the lowlands of local creeks and rivers.   On top of this, accessible reserves of coal and oil and other minerals had been discovered in the vicinity.

The Tiger's backyard had moved to the front burner in terms of its readiness for exploitation and development.   Their area was still too remote and rough to be easily accessed by land, which meant that access by rail was the final ingredient necessary to make settlement possible in what until then had been an area too isolated for practical uses.   This problem was solved in 1905, when the Muskogee Union Railway (later called the Missouri, Oklahoma, and Gulf Railroad—the MO&G—announced plans for an extension into their area from nearby Muskogee.

It was at this point that a group of well-funded investors—Charles E. Davis, Ira E. Davis, Noah B. Davis, Elmer E. Schock, and J. H. Osborne—joined forces to create a company for the express purpose of developing land around where the Tiger family lived.   The investors hired J. M. Kinyon and G. E. Carney to launch their new venture and handle its day-to-day operations.   They made Kinyon and Carney the "exclusive" land agents of their new business, which they named the Hoffman Townsite and Realty Company.

In January of 1905, only a matter of months before the new railroad extension was completed, Kinyon and Carney found a location for a new town in the area they had been charged with developing, a site that, until then, had been nothing more than an isolated Indian settlement. The new town was to be built on a plot of 160 acres they bought from its original freedman allottee, a man by the name of George Hawkins. The Tiger's land was only a short distance away.

As soon as they had the site in their hands, the developers plotted it into residential and commercial lots and put it up for sale. The new town was opened to buyers in August of 1905, the same month the rail line to the site was completed by the regional railway company. They named the town Hoffman, in honor of William Hoffman, one of the vice presidents of the railroad company.

As soon as rail service was extended to the town site, there was an immediate boom in terms of the number of homestead claim filings and other forms of land purchasing and use. Speculators bought land with the hope of being able to resell it for immediate short-term profits, while others bought with long-term investment in mind.

Land churning was quite common, and it was a perfectly legal practice. Investors and settlers alike were unabashedly interested in full and immediate exploitation of local natural resources such as timber, oil, and coal, with the intent of making as much as possible, as quickly as possible. Land acquisition records for the years that followed show that the more astute developers were careful to buy up, whenever they could, mineral rights as well as raw land.

The new Town of Hoffman was officially incorporated on August 29, 1905, while the land on which it was founded was still part of Oklahoma Indian Territory. It was launched from the beginning for the purpose of commercial development, and the first lot at the town site was sold on that same date. The State of Oklahoma and, in turn, McIntosh County, the county it wound up in, didn't come into being until over two years later, on November 16, 1907. In 1918, political jurisdiction over the town was transferred to Okmulgee County.

From the day it was incorporated, land investment opportunities in and around Hoffman were aggressively promoted to all comers. Potential buyers were drawn in from all over the country, but most came in from the nearby states of Arkansas, Kansas, Mississippi, and Missouri. Several of the men involved in the town site development company either already were or soon became among the first residents of the town; thus, they had vested interests in seeing it grow and prosper. Any land they didn't use for their own ventures was, of course, sold for whatever personal profit could be reaped. In turn, those who bought these plots wasted no time in marking them up for further speculative resale.

The developers were aggressive and unreservedly expansive in terms of promoting their newly formed town site.   Touting the area they intended to develop in glowing terms, it was described exactly as follows in their promotional literature:

Hoffman, I.T., is at present a town of about 500 population, located on the M. O. & G. Railroad about 35 miles southwest of Muskogee and 12 miles east of Henryetta in the center of the Creek Nation, Indian Territory.   It is surrounded by the most fertile and productive farm prairie and timberlands in the Territory, which is adapted to all the cereals of the North and also cotton, the king of crops in the South.   It is located on a parallel west of Fort Smith, Arkansas, which gives us a climate that has neither extremes of heat or cold. This is demonstrated by the scenic effects produced by the profusion of which all flowers and shrubbery grow, and as a fruit country our soil is unsurpassed.

With these surroundings we have a country we can well feel proud of, and as a location for a town Hoffman has many advantages that will attract the prospective homeseeker and speculator, as we have an ideal location for a tile and brick plant and a material that as a clay will stand the inspection of the most skeptical, and we are located accessible to the best coal fields in the Indian Territory.   We are also accessible to the Deep Fork of the Canadian River, which would supply any demand for water for manufacturing purposes; and being well timbered with all the harder growths of marketable timber which would supply an unlimited demand for fuel for manufacturing purposes.

Since the time of opening, the town has grown beyond the expectation of all who reside here, and all who visit the place are very agreeably surprised at the marvelous growth of the town and the unsurpassed quality of the soil, that insures the town a good and permanent support. Any desiring a location of any kind or who is looking for a place of investment will receive the most courteous attention by visiting or addressing the Hoffman Townsite & Realty Company.

At some point during these early years, a newspaper called The Hoffman Herald opened for business. The editor, a man by the name of O. E. O'Bleness, who, of course, had vested interests of his own in the town, published a regular series of articles that further touted the many attractions of the new town site, its people, and its many new buildings. On April 5, 1905, he wrote:

To begin at the beginning would be somewhat like writing the history before the historian were born, but even this would be possible where the landmarks were so plain as they were when the writer of these lines first set his foot on the townsite of where Hoffman now stands.   Our first visit to the town was in October of last year, and at that time it consisted only of a few trading places and a very few small dwellings, but after looking over the surrounding country, it took us only a short time to arrive at the conclusion that it was just such as would someday support a thriving city of several thousand people.

Whether it was by accident or otherwise, it matters not, but it is a fact that the townsite people could not have made a better selection for the location of a town than right here where Hoffman now stands. This land is rich, well-watered bottomland and capable of growing a profitable crop of almost anything in the vegetable, fruit or cereal line.   To the north of the town lies hundreds, yes, thousands of acres of rolling, black sandy prairie land covered with a growth of bluestem grass from three to five feet high, which is only wanting the attention of the industrious farmer when it will produce crops that will return him a hundred fold for his efforts.

In fact, all the land surrounding the town is rich agricultural land, excepting a range of small hills to the south and west, and they are underlaid with heavy deposits of good coal and vast lakes of oil.   In fact, only seven miles west on the M. O. & G Railway this coal deposit is now being successfully worked and it is only reasonable to presume that at no distant date a *profitable coal and oil field will be opened almost within the town limits of Hoffman. Yes, we might go on and write columns regarding the country but the above is sufficient to show that the country around Hoffman when properly farmed is sufficient to support a city of several thousand.*

If there was money to be made, civic booster Mr. O'Bleness, an objective journalist if there ever was one, obviously wanted to be in on the action. Under the circumstances, no one would have blamed him for wanting to try. In any event, it was his brand of commentary that drew new people to the area, each one of them intent upon cashing in on the opportunity that was to be had out in the territory, just like the writer whose words had pulled them there.

— 11 —

HOFFMAN
GETS SETTLED

AS SOON AS LAND in the Indian Territory around where Early and Bonnie Tiger lived became available to outsiders, interested parties from neighboring states started making inspection visits to the town site and surrounding area, and some of them decided to make investments, buy acreage, or open a business as a means of taking their own bite of the apple. Purchasing land in or around new towns like Hoffman was considered a great opportunity for those who were interested in entrepreneurship, homesteading, ranching or other forms of business or professional activity. Land in the area had become hot property, and Hoffman was a farm town with a future that looked promising and bright.

The original residents of the Hoffman area—most of them mixed or full- blooded Creek Indians and runaway blacks and their descendants, along with a smattering of illegal or quasi-legal white settlers— were, of course, immediately and dramatically affected by the changes that were occurring. They were all but surrounded by newly arrived investors, speculators, and settlers who were eager to cash in on any opportunity the area had to offer. For natives and settlers alike, it had to have been a heady and unsettling experience.

The new arrivals began to construct homes, create farms and ranches, open new businesses, build banks and churches and other private and commercial buildings, and develop the basic government services that were needed to meet civic needs. All of them were anxious to get about the business of making money in their new and exciting hometown.

Most of the new people came in as true settlers, folks who had dreams of owning their own land and cultivating farms, building up ranches, starting an independent trade or craft business, or opening retail stores or other commercial enterprises. The great majority of them were hard-working people, individuals in search of a good economic opportunity. They had been drawn to the area by the spirit of adventure and their desire for prosperity. Dreams like these made the area a magnet, a lodestone many couldn't resist.

Along with those who showed up in or around the area encompassing the new town site as true settlers or honest investors were some who were better described as opportunists and gamblers. Many arrived there in search of a chance to make a quick financial killing, and they didn't have many scruples about how they went about doing it. Speculators, schemers, scam artists, and out-and-out crooks descended upon the relatively naive and often illiterate native Indians and blacks who lived in and around Hoffman, all of them hoping to make money through any marginally legal—and sometimes flagrantly illegal—means they could employ without being thrown in jail. Lots of documentation exists to prove this today, but no help was available to their victims, not back when it was needed.

Using one unscrupulous approach or another, schemers did whatever they could think of to defraud Indian and black land allottees out of all or part of the value of their property. In some cases, white trustees appointed by the courts to "help" minor or orphaned Indian and black land allottees, for example, bought land from them for a pittance or defrauded them of its true value through various legal but highly unethical means. Some of the recipients of their so-called help ended up out on the street, literally as well as figuratively, without a dollar to their name.

What made matters worse for locals and new arrivals alike was that banking and investment companies of their time were essentially unregulated entities. With next to no oversight or operating guidelines to restrict their activities, the public was not always well protected from unethical business practices, fraud, embezzle-ment, or overt criminal activity. Owners of banks, as an example, were among those who speculated freely and legally on local properties and business ventures of their own, often unintentionally—but in some cases intentionally—subsuming the interests of their depositors. It is well known that serious problems are far more likely to crop up when the assets of individuals and businesses are commingled with the personal assets of the owners of a financial institution, but the practice was common during this highly chaotic interval.

The Tigers were not directly affected by the provisions of the Dawes Act of 1887 until 1904, when Early and his daughter found themselves beneficiaries of the federal government's land allotment program. Early was deeded the standard 160-acre allotment that was awarded to married men, while his daughter was deeded 80 acres. Early's wife Etta had, in her husband's words, "run off" years earlier, but that didn't matter, since wives weren't allotted anything. All that mattered to Early was that he wound up with a land allotment of 240 acres under his control, some of which was alongside of the Deep Fork River and highly valued for farming.

One more federal government-initiated change that had an impact on Bonnie Tiger was that she was assigned a "full and proper" (meaning white) name when she received her allotment. A middle name was assigned to her because administrators of the allotment program had been directed to record full names for anyone to whom government land was allotted, legal names having been considered necessary for government census and record-keeping purposes.

Those who had only partial white names were assigned new ones on the spot, as their allotments were awarded. With free land being doled out like manna from heaven, those who had no full white name felt no great desire to question the practice. Not only did the assignment of new names seem fair and reasonable under the circumstances, most of the recipients of new names were pleased to get them. It was in this way that, from then on, Bonnie Tiger became legally known as Bonnie Marie Tiger and Early Tiger became Early Ray Tiger. Even so, everyone still referred to her as Tiger, and he was still referred to as Early.

Had it not been for her father's interference, having received an allotment of 80 acres would have been an exciting event in Tiger's life. The land was worth money, now that so many outsiders had become interested in investing or settling thereabouts. In her case, though, the award didn't lead to any changes at all in her life.

"You take care of the house," her father ordered, "and I'll take care of our business." Having been conditioned since childhood to accede to his every command, it didn't even occur to her to challenge him. She knew what would happen if she talked back in any way, so she kept her mouth shut and did what she was told. For her, life went on as before, as if there had never been an allotment program.

In contrast, Early intended to cash in on their good fortune as quickly as he could make it happen. He was so tired of being broke and struggling to get by that he had no intention of sharing any benefit that might be derived from the sale of their land with his daughter. To his way of thinking, she already had more than she really needed. Leasing out or, if he could find a way to get around government restrictions, selling off the land was exactly what he hoped to do —and for his benefit alone. His own wants and needs were all that mattered to him: He didn't give more than a few passing thoughts to what Tiger may have wanted or needed.

Early and other resident natives did not fully appreciate how their vulnerability skyrocketed when they ended up on the list of allotment recipients, making them prey for whites who were ready and willing to separate them from their property by means ranging from the abuse of court-appointed guardianships to blatant fraud. Early and Tiger didn't realize it, but they had become ripe, practical targets for all sorts of scammers and schemers.

Their unique circumstances of isolation, poverty, and having little education or political awareness had turned Indian residents of the territory into highly vulnerable human beings, and Early and Tiger were no exceptions. In their case, the problem was worsened by their miserable home conditions, in that their own discontent made them even more susceptible to the persuasions of con artists than they had been all along. Tiger had minimal understanding of the forces that were afoot, and Early was more than ready to take advantage of any opportunity for extracting immediate cash out of their newly acquired land that came his way.

Early's household had long been a plum ripe for the picking, but it was having received a valuable tract of allotment land that brought the fruit to market. Being taken advantage of was not an unusual consequence of Indian land ownership during this interval; many Indians were victimized in this way—men, women, and children alike. For some Indians, placing an asset with a cash value in their hands was, on occasion, like pouring fuel onto an open fire. Like the Tigers, many of them were totally unprepared to deal with all the various forms of devious crookedness that came their way.

All that saved the Tiger household from outside exploitation even before the allotment program was that they had had nothing worthy of being exploited. If they had had any such assets, there is no doubt that Early would have sold them, without thinking through the long-term effects that such a sale might have on him or on his daughter. Now, though, they had in their possession an asset most certainly worthy of exploitation.

Lots of other Indian residents of the territory were in the same boat as the Tigers. In this sense, at least, Early and his daughter were equals among their peers, despite their marginal status within the community. In what for many Indians was a highly significant way, their circumstances had changed, and plenty of outsiders had taken notice. In the Tiger family's case, the hammer did eventually fall, but not in the way those who were familiar with the dynamics that existed between Early and his daughter would have anticipated. Tiger was the member of the family who ended up being exploited, not, as any reasonable observer of their household would have expected, her shiftless excuse for a father.

— 12 —

TIGER'S FIRST
SALVATION

WHEN EARLY TIGER unexpectedly passed away in his sleep on March 17, 1904, shortly after he and his daughter were awarded their tracts of allotment land, she considered his death a form of salvation—not immediately, but after thinking about it for a while. Tiger didn't mourn for her father's passing, that's for sure. His wife couldn't mourn for him, either, since she wasn't around to do so. She had disappeared from the face of the earth long before, very likely, in the opinion of those who knew them, by her husband's own hand.

The news of Early Tiger's sudden death came as no great surprise to any of the local authority figures who had had to deal with the ill effects of his drunken, troublesome behavior over the years, but it was initially very shocking to his long-suffering daughter. Tiger's first reaction to the news was utter disbelief; her father been such a dominant presence in her life for so long that she had trouble imagining his being gone.

Something as huge as the possibility of his dying had never even as much as occurred to her, which was why the news that it had, in fact, happened knocked her back on her heels for a while. Could it really be true, she wondered, pinching herself to make sure she wasn't dreaming, that he would no longer be the central reality of her daily life? Was it possible that such a wonderful thing had happened?

For her, his malevolent presence had long since become the worst aspect of living in their home—worse even than the seasonal heat or cold or the aggressive mosquitoes or any of the other forms of discomfort and privation that had been part and parcel of her everyday existence. Her life had been cheerless for so long it was hard to imagine that an actual positive change might have taken place. It took a while to process what happened, and she was not able to breathe a first great sigh of relief until she finally did.

All that came as a surprise to local authorities was that Early Tiger had died of natural causes in his own bed, as opposed to being stabbed in an alley or shot in a barroom brawl or something else along those lines. That was the kind of end they had expected for him.

Immediately after his passing, however, was not the right time for them to blather on about the circumstances of his death or how he had misspent his life. A much more important matter needed immediate at this juncture; namely, what should be done on behalf of his 21-year-old daughter Bonnie? What, everyone wondered, was the girl going to do, now that she had been left alone in the world? With her father dead and her mother, if not also dead, no longer on the scene, they knew that Tiger was now the only living member of what every one of them had begun to think of as one of the most ill-fated family they'd ever dealt with.

Tiger, too, after she finally accepted that her father's death was for real, saw that she had to take fresh look at her situation. Now that she was on her own, she had to decide what she wanted to do with herself. This was easy to say but hard to do, given that she was not yet fully adjusted to the enormity of what had happened.

After carefully thinking things over, she concluded that her only practical option was to continue living in the same reclusive way she had when her father was alive. He wouldn't be there, she thought to herself, but her own daily life would otherwise be much the same. Her primary concern had to do with how she and she alone would have to find a way to make a living off the meager belongings he left behind. His home and possessions belonged to her now, and it would be up to her to make the best of them.

Her father's estate consisted of a scraggly and unkempt plot of communal land, a run-down and unpainted old wood frame house, a collection of shoddy furniture, a nearly tumbled-down barn, a dilapidated old wagon, a couple of spavined horses, a few rangy cows and sheep, a gaggle of equally rangy hogs, an assortment of chickens, guinea hens, geese, and ducks, and a small stash of cash she found hidden at the back of one of his dresser drawers. Beyond these meager items, Tiger was left with no more real property than a limited wardrobe and the clothes that were on her back.

All the basics required for her to continue living a normal rural existence were in place, even if every item he left behind was either shabby or near to being on its last legs. The lump sum value of all his assets taken together would not have amounted to much, but to Tiger, who had never had anything she could call own, it seemed like quite a lot.

She didn't know at that point what to do about all the acres of allotment land that now belonged to her—the land her father had ordered her to think of as being his and his alone. All the land was hers now, and she realized it was her most valuable possession. She had no immediate idea what to do with it, nor did she have any concept of what it might be worth. All she knew was that it would be worth *something*, especially now that so many outsiders were moving into the area and Hoffman was growing so much. *More great news*, she said to herself.

Cashing in on the value of the land would have enabled her to move if she had wanted to, but Tiger was unable to envision any other approach to life than to keep on keeping on, living where she was, in the same way as she had in the past. Having been kept out of school and raised in as much isolation within their community as her father could manage, the life of an isolated and impoverished Indian was all she knew. At this point, therefore, she didn't expect any more out of life than more of the same.

For the moment, one overwhelmingly welcome thought had lodged in her mind and taken precedence over every other issue that needed to be dealt with: No matter what problems had to be solved in the wake of her father's passing, her daily life was sure to be much less miserable than it had been while he was alive! Under his control, she had had no choice but to jump at his command. Now, though, she would no longer have to live in fear of his drunken bullying, threats, and eccentricities, nor would it be necessary for her to wait on him hand and foot. Better still, never again would she have to put up with the fear of being terrorized on a whim when she did or done not do something he considered deserving of punishment. *Nothing*, she exclaimed aloud to herself, *could be better than that!*

The more she thought about the freedom that was going to be hers to enjoy, the more excited she became. *Praise the Lord: Will wonders never cease!* Realizing that she no longer had to worry about being treated like a criminal in her own home wasn't merely exciting; it was exhilarating!

As if she were a prisoner unexpectedly released after long years of confinement, her euphoria knew no bounds! Tiger was absolutely thrilled by her change of circumstances, even though that was a decidedly unusual reaction for someone who had only recently lost a parent. *Why in the world should I be upset over the death of a father like mine?* she asked herself, after thinking back over how badly he had used and abused her over the years. The truth of the matter, she realized, was that she most definitely was *not* sorry he was gone; she was not sorry in the least.

Oh, she knew she would have to deal with all the many practical realities that living alone would entail, but she was confident that she would be able to manage them without any undue problems. For years, every lick of work that had been done in their household had been done by her anyway; her father had hardly ever lifted a finger. For this reason, the thought of having to get by on her own was not the least bit daunting.

In more specific terms, she was confident that she would be able to get by on milk and eggs provided by their rangy domestic animals, vegetables harvested out of their poorly kept garden, any fish or game that could be trapped or killed, nuts and fruit and berries that could be gathered from down in the Deep Fork River bottom, and whatever forms of assistance the federal government would dole out to the

Indians of her area. Those sources of nourishment, she took for granted, would be more than enough to meet her needs.

Suddenly ending up alone in the way she had would have unnerved and threatened many young women, but her new circumstances didn't bother Tiger in the slightest. Enraptured by thoughts of all the many pleasures she expected to flow from being out from under her father's domineering thumb, she looked forward to trying to get by alone. The real truth, as a matter of fact, was that she could hardly wait to get on with it.

So, after contemplating her prospects for a while, Tiger made it clear to those who had offered to help her that that was what she intended to do: She was going to live alone, do things her own way, get by on her own, and survive in the same way that she had in the past. She didn't want or need help from anyone, she said. She was convinced that she could take care of herself.

After making her intentions clear to one and all, she launched into running her newly inherited household as she saw fit, reporting to no one, catering to no one, and, best of all, without having to cower down before a man who treated her more like an unpaid domestic servant than as a daughter. Love had never existed in their household, so she didn't miss something she never had. The bully was gone, and she was so pleased she felt like dancing in the street!

She found it exciting to be able to set her own pace and call her own shots when it came to dealing with matters of the moment. She flat out *loved* her freedom. She had begun a new life, one that seemed too good to be true!

From a financial standpoint, Bonnie Tiger's lot in life was much better than it had been earlier. Not only had she become the proud owner of 240 acres of allotment land, but she had also been awarded a dependable government subsistence check and a regular allowance of staples. For the first time in her life, her Indian heritage was paying off in a tangible way.

At the same time, though, her social status within the community wasn't any more elevated than it had been before, even though she now had real property and other assets and advantages to do with as she pleased. Her neighbors and others still thought of her as a woman with an unsavory reputation, and she knew it. If anything, they thought even less of her than before, at least to her way of thinking. Social elevation was what she longed for, more than anything else.

The routine gossip that was part and parcel of everyday life in a small community had made her as well known to new settlers as she was to nearly every other resident of the area, Indians, whites, and blacks alike. Hoffman was a town where everybody knew everybody, and, sadly for Tiger, most residents had come to think of her as an intemperate and unruly person rather than what she really was—an eccentric, solely due to how she had been raised. They knew that she'd been brought up under conditions bad enough to have broken the back as well as the will of anyone, and it was commonly thought that exactly that had happened to her. Nobody thought of her a solid marital prospect, that's for sure. Her many personal hang-ups and quirks, everyone agreed, virtually guaranteed that becoming a good partner in a normal marriage just wasn't in her cards.

Tragically, Tiger's own behavior as she grew further into womanhood only strengthen-ed the widely held conviction that she was damaged goods. Most of what neighbors and other residents of the community had to say about her was, regrettably, true. Having been raised through being whipped into blind and fearful obedience by her drunken father, once she was on her own and out from under his control, she was forever resentful of all authority, whether it was rightful and legitimate or not. She was particularly suspicious and hostile toward men, especially Indian men, because they made her think of her father. Her neighbors were aware of her various hang-ups and eccentricities, and that's why so many believed all things would continue to go badly for her.

Life was confusing for most Indians when her change of circumstances took place, but they had to have been even more confusing for a young single woman like Tiger, who had only a tenuous grip on things anyway. In her day, women everywhere lived in a man's world, and the effects of this reality were even highly pronounced in her neck of the woods. In her context, it was a real problem for a woman to live with a chip on her shoulder. Her own attitude, it must be said, made things more difficult than they had to be.

Because Tiger was a young woman who had a considerable amount of weight on her shoulders, she was especially prone to grasping for easy answers to difficult problems. In this sense, people said, she was much like her parents, in that this same inclination had kept them in trouble all the time. Neighbors and others sensed she was desperately looking for a makeover, for any easy path she could find to improve her dismal social standing. To them, she was a woman with a ready-made reputation, a woman on the make, and it didn't matter whether she'd come by it honestly or not.

— 13 —

TIGER IS OVERCOME BY CABIN FEVER AND LONELINESS

MUCH TO EVERYONE'S SURPRISE, Tiger was able to live on own for eight long years. She was so thrilled to be away from her father that most of those years of living by herself flew by without any doubt on her part. She had convinced herself that she would be able to continue living alone forever.

Gradually, though, as those who really understood what was going on with her had predicted, things began to change. To her annoyance, unexplainable feelings of discontent began to set in. Try as she might to dispel these aggravating notions, she found that she could not. Living alone, she had discovered, was not going to remain as easy as she thought it would.

Her change of attitude did not take place until she lived alone for many years, but she eventually figured out that wanting with all her heart to live happily ever after would never shield her from the realities of human existence. Sensing rather than having been taught or having consciously learned that people—and more particularly, young single women—aren't naturally inclined to live alone, she was overwhelmed by forces she had no way of anticipating.   Those forces were cabin fever and its inevitable companion, human loneliness.

As the walls of the rundown home she inherited from her father slowly began to close in on her, longings she had not imagined, did not understand, and over which she had no control began to dominate her every thought.   She tried with all her might to force them out of mind, but even after giving it her best effort she could not manage to do so.   In what seemed like a matter of months but really was many long years, she found it difficult to think about anything else.

Living within what began to feel like a confined space had the effect of focusing far too much attention on what was missing in her life.   The fact that she was an extremely maladjusted person did not lessen these feelings; if anything, it made them even more intense.   Before long, she realized that, if changes were not made in the way she was living, it was conceivable that she might go altogether off the rails.   The silence by which she was surrounded, as silence is wont to do, dominated her every thought. All she could think of was how quiet things were and how lonely she felt.

Meeting her basic material needs, she finally realized, had never been her major problem; she had been able to deal with all that without any undue effort, just as she had imagined she could.   No, her real problem was that she, in the same way as everyone else, needed normal human companionship, someone to center life around and add meaning to her existence. That, she had discovered, as all people eventually do, is what life is all about. She had heard it said on many occasions that people do not live by bread alone, but, up to this this point in life, she had never as much as imagined that this proverb applied to her in the same way as it did to everyone else.

In Tiger's case, however, developing an open-eyed awareness of the pressing problem she had to face up to in no way diminished how difficult it was going to be to do anything about it. That, she recognized, would be a whole different matter. Dealing with a problem of its kind would require getting involved in activities she didn't know the first thing about. It would involve getting off into entirely new turf for her, and she knew it.

Growing up under the absolute control of an authoritarian, heavy-handed, intimidating father had not left much time for her to worry about the softer side of life, since being at his beck and call around the clock had been the whole reason for her existence. While she had happily welcomed his absence at first, the silence that replaced the old man's constant bellowing had finally beaten her down.

Getting along well in the world, she had discovered, was going to be much more a matter of learning how to deal with her personal longings than of meeting her needs for basic personal wherewithal. The latter, compared to the former, was an absolute piece of cake. Merely thinking about having to deal with matters of this personal kind aroused a sense of dread in her.

As every person sooner or later does, she had figured out that living on her own and keeping her own company would never be enough to make her truly happy. People, she felt in her heart, need other people, and that's the way it is, whether they want it to be that way or not. It was something of an epiphany to realize that this was just as true for her as it was for others; up until then, she thought she was different and that she would be happy to be set apart forever. Now, though, it had become clear that she had been wrong all along. She had considered herself different, but she really wasn't, at least not in this sensitive area.

Tiger, to say the least, was way behind the curve when it came to dealing with matters of the heart. That this was the case came as no great revelation to those who knew her, since it was common knowledge that she'd been kept out of school during her early years and brought up in near isolation from anyone outside of her own neurotic family. Having been raised more like an indentured servant than a typical child, she hadn't learned most of life's most fundamental lessons. Due to seldom ever having interacted with others in social settings of any kind, she had no inter-personal skills to speak of. She was about as socially inept and back woodsy as a young woman could be.

Tiger had summoned up a general but limited understanding of her own personal problem, but she still had no concept of how to go about dealing with it. She had no idea where or how to begin. Figuring out how to dispel the confusion brought on by the new cravings that had cropped up in her life was going to be one of the most difficult problems she had ever had to deal with. For any young woman, dealing with questions of this kind can be perplexing, but for her it was doubly so, since she was not a typical young woman. She was anything but normal, and that's what made contending with her predicament so daunting.

Living alone most definitely had turned out to be nothing like the rosy and carefree experience she imagined it would be, but, again, not for the basic reason she had worried about early on. Thriving on a day-to-day basis, she had discerned, was going to be much more a matter of figuring out how to contend with her loneliness than on making sure her material needs were met.

Her father's roars and demands had filled up her empty spaces in the past, but now all of that was gone. She didn't miss her old life, of course, but the absence of it had left a new problem in its stead. A vacuum had been created, and Tiger felt it acutely. Not knowing how to go about meeting her intangible personal needs was turning her inside out.

After having emotionally declined to the point of being about ready to jump out of her own skin, Tiger finally decided that something absolutely had to be done about how lonely she felt. Things couldn't go on the way they were. The despair that hovered over her like a malignant force would never go away if she continued living like she was. She knew that brooding and stewing was different from attempting a solution, but at the same time she also knew that any solution she came up with would be the subject of intense and merciless scrutiny on the part of her intrusive neighbors. To her, it seemed as if they criticized everything, not matter what she said or did.

In the end, she concluded that it really didn't matter what others might think of what-ever approach she chose for dealing with her situation. She had become too troubled to care. If she ended up embarrassing herself, so what. The choice before her was either to try in some way to deal with what ailed her, or to go off the deep end altogether. From where she sat, her dilemma was as straightforward as that.

Tiger knew she had to get something going, and that's all there was to it. Even if she failed and ended up subjected to a new round of censure and derision, her neighbors couldn't make her feel any worse than she already felt.   She knew they'd scrutinize and then scathingly criticize whatever she might say or do, since they never tired of finding new aspects of her lifestyle to ridicule.   Niceties, she decided, were not going to help her; she had no choice but to take proactive steps on her own behalf, not later, but immediately.

— 14 —

A DEBUT IN
THE HINTERLANDS

AFTER HER PERSPECTIVE changed from passive acceptance to go-for-broke aggressiveness, Tiger tore into her problem by devising an approach to dealing with it that most impartial observers would have described as being too far beyond the pale for her time and place. It isn't uncommon for lonely people to occasionally move forward as if they are wearing blinders, and at this point extreme loneliness caused Tiger to join their desperate ranks. Doing something, she had concluded, would be much better than doing nothing, no matter what adverse effects it might have. Besides, she had already tried doing nothing, and that had gotten her nowhere.

Implementation of the course of action she settled on began with pulling together as much cash money as she could raise, starting with selling off to neighbors one of her pair of old horses, one of her two equally over-the-hill cows, and a few of the hogs and piglets she had raised by breeding those she had inherited from her father. When these proceeds were pooled with the cash that had been found hidden at the back of one of his dresser drawers, she had enough in hand to move on to the second step of her plan.

At this point, she hitched her remaining old horse to her even older wagon and headed off toward town. She had done the same thing on many occasions with her father before he died and afterwards, whenever she had to replenish her supplies of salt, flour, coffee, and other staples. All that made this trip different was that it wasn't being made for the purpose of buying commodities; it was being made for the specific purpose of setting herself up to pursue what she expected to be a whole new future. This time around, what she had in mind was getting set up to market *herself!*

Her first stop of the morning was not for groceries but to peruse the apparel on display at the largest of Hoffman's general merchandise stores. As soon as the proprietor noted her frenetic intentness on spending a good part of the money she had in hand, he happily guided her through the mechanics of buying certain items for cash and for ordering others out of the mail-order catalog kept at the sales counter.

Working with the storekeeper, Tiger looked through pictures in the catalog to select and order a few Tulsa–town fancy dresses, a pair of stylish of high-top lace-up black leather shoes, a few pairs of long stockings, a pair of matching gloves, and a parasol. She left the store as pleased as punch with what she had ordered, even more pleased than the lucky merchant.

From the general store, she went down to the Ideal Hat Shop on Main Street to buy a stylish new hat to go with her classy new dresses. Even though it wasn't a big place, Hoffman had its own hat store. It was fashionable during the 1910s for everyone, male or female, to wear a hat, and Tiger, who had never worn anything on her head but stringy hair, knew she needed to put an end to that.

From the hat shop, she stopped by to visit with a lady who cut and dressed hair out of her home, where she pre-scheduled an appointment to coincide with the promised delivery date of the new outfitting she had on order. She knew she would need some help in this area, since good grooming and dressing fashionably was something she hadn't been able to pay attention to in the past. Until this point in life, she had worn nothing but ragged and shapeless flour sack dresses and devoted only a minimal amount of effort to taking care of her hair or making up her face.

Her final stop of the day was at Frank Wilson's Livery Stable, where she pre-arranged the rental of an attractive light buckboard for use during the series of trips back to town she planned to make in the future. The ragged old hand-me-down wagon her father left behind wasn't suitable for what she had in mind.

As soon as her new finery came in, Tiger intended to put herself out there. On holidays and at selected public events, she intended to make herself as visible as possible. Enough, Tiger had decided, was enough; it was long past time for her to break out of the life of isolation she had been living and let everyone know that she was single and available. No man would find his way to her door without knowing who she was, that was for sure.

If she wanted to bring about a change in her way of life, Tiger knew that she had to take decisive action on her own behalf, since no one would ever do it for her. *Whether I make a mistake or not*, she said aloud to herself, *I have to do whatever is needed to change what's going on in my life and, hopefully, improve my own future.* Forcing change to happen, as she saw it, was her only way out.

So, from that point forward, that's what she did: On any and every occasion that presented half a reason for her to do so, she headed back into town. Dressed up in her new outfits, she sashayed from venue to venue on her fancy rented buckboard, wearing her stylish new clothing, smiling all the while, and bantering with any eligible (and, in some cases, ineligible) members of the other sex who would talk with her. Flaunting in equal measure her new clothing as well as her own availability, she made sure that every man in town knew exactly who she was.

It goes without saying that many of her conservative neighbors didn't think highly of her new approach to life. What they thought, as a matter of fact, was that yet another member of her crazy family had taken a dive off the deep end, since no socially conscious woman in their setting would have as much as even dreamt of so openly and aggressively flaunting her availability.

Carrying on in what was thought to be an obviously wanton manner caused neighbors who had only pitied her while she was stuck with her drunken excuse for a father to look down on Tiger in a whole new way Criticizing her in the harshest of terms, she became the subject of even more disapproval and vitriolic gossip than in the past. That others thought of what she was doing in this way was too bad, since it was a complete misinterpretation of what really was afoot. Tiger hadn't become a floozy over night; all she wanted was to meet one good man. Her problem was that she had a very poor understanding of socially appropriate ways of making it happen.

There's no doubt about it, her neighbors sagely opined: "That silly girl is going to make a serious mistake before long, if not of one kind, then of another, in the same way that her sorry mother did before her. Her behavior," they said to one another, "is living proof that the apple doesn't fall far from the tree." Because it was common knowledge that Tiger was more like a lamb before wolves than a typical young woman, they took for granted that it wouldn't be long before the axe would fall. "What a shame," they said among themselves, "but what in the world could any of them do about it!"

On her part, Tiger began to swing between bouts of euphoria brought on by how bold and free it felt to ride about town on a flashy buckboard while dressed in fancy new clothing and episodes of painful depression that sprang up as she became increasingly aware of how low her neighbors thought she had fallen. She tried to keep up a good front while she was out and about, but, as might be imagined, it was not long before she began to think less of herself than ever before. *Not a thing I do*, she whimpered during quiet moments, *ever turns out right!*

— 15 —

TIGER'S
SECOND SALVATION

ANGRY AND DISGUSTED with her neighbors, her town, and, for that matter, the whole miserable Indian Territory, Tiger fell into yet another round of debilitating weepiness. The sense of weariness and lassitude that so often accompanied her battle with this ongoing problem really pulled her down, until Tiger found herself back on the verge of a whole new episode of unbearable depression. Thinking that nothing would ever get better for her, she fell into a terrible state of mind.

Then, just as she was teetering on the edge of giving up hope of ever finding love, another hugely significant event occurred in Tiger's life: A genuinely interested and eligible man appeared in her field of vision. For the very first time, she realized, she was being courted. Even though—or more accurately *because*—she was scraping an emotional rock bottom when they met, she was immediately taken by the tall, good-looking white man who was known within their community as the Colonel but whose real name was George Jackson Caine.

Precisely how and exactly when Tiger and George first met and became acquainted is not known, but somehow or another Tiger had made it happen.   Coming together during low points in their respective lives didn't seem to matter, since they got on well from the beginning.   He seemed genuinely pleased to have met her, and she was even more pleased to have met him.

George explained that he was but one of many settlers who had moved out to the territory to take advantage of the low-priced farmland that was available near the new town.   He moved there, he said, in search of a fresh start, in the same way as his many counterparts.   Then, he said, before three years passed by, both his wife and child had died of unknown illnesses, leaving him a childless widower. That, he claimed, was when he decided that he couldn't bear to stay out on his farm any longer. Shortly afterwards, he sold the land he'd owned on the outskirts of town and moved into Hoffman proper.   Tiger, as would be imagined, couldn't see any reason to hold any of this against him, especially after picking up on the fact that he was after the same thing she was—a fresh start. She was aware of there being a lot more unattached men than unattached women in their area, but she didn't fully appreciate that some of those men were far more appropriately described as *opportunity seekers* than *legitimate settlers*.   Her suitor portrayed himself as having been one of the latter, when in truth he was much more the former. Because Tiger couldn't see that, she bought into every word the Colonel said.

She'd talked with many of the men in the area, but none of them had come across as well as handsome George, nor did any of them pay as much attention to her as he did. Most of the men she'd gotten involved with had turned out to be grippers and grabbers interested in only one thing, and what they were interested in was the opposite of what she was after. She wasn't used to being the object of an eligible male's positive attention, and, now that she was, she liked it a great deal. To her, in fact, it meant everything.

Unsurprisingly, Tiger concluded that the man everyone referred to as "Colonel Caine" was someone who had an excellent chance of moving up in the world. He was already gainfully employed as one of two barbers at Harmony's Barbershop, and he openly spoke of being in search of a bigger and better opportunity to delve into at some point down the road. Tiger didn't hold that against him, either; in fact, it made her think all the better of him, because she thought that way herself.

To describe Tiger's impression of the Colonel more pointedly, she saw him as a star to whom one's wagon could profitably be hitched. There's no doubt about it, she said to herself; *George Caine is most definitely the type of man I've been looking for.* From her perspective, the plan she'd implemented to "put herself out there" had worked exactly as she had hoped. Until she acted on her own behalf, she'd never even been around an eligible man, much less actively courted by one, and that such a striking, vigorous, bold young white man was paying close attention to her was more than enough to sweep her off her feet.

From the Colonel's pragmatic perspective, however, their relationship was far more prosaic and much more calculated than Tiger had enough experience to imagine. He had been through interactions like theirs before, not once but on multiple occasions. Tiger saw George Caine as her second deliverance, but, to all outward appearances, it seemed to others that he saw her as more as a means to an end than anything else.

Less than three months after their first meeting, the happy couple decided to tie the marital knot. It was a bold move for each of them, but it was far bolder for her than for him. Because he had been married before, he knew what he was getting into, while she, although mature in terms of chronological age, had never even had a boyfriend. They ignored all of that and made it official anyway, in a formal union conducted by Justice of the Peace Bert Osborn on May 12, 1913.

It was in this way that George Jackson Caine, *the Colonel*, met and wedded his Creek Indian wife Bonnie Marie Tiger. Because it had happened on the heels of low points in both their lives, it wasn't surprising that outsiders conjectured about whether they had gotten married for love alone, for money alone, or for a combination thereof. It really wasn't anybody's business, of course, but that wasn't enough to keep speculation about their motives from running rampant. From the moment neighbors and other residents of the community became aware of their marriage, that very thing was what happened.

People knew their marriage didn't mean the same thing to Tiger as it did to George, to say the very least. To her, marriage was an opportunity to fill a gaping void in her life as well as a means of reaching a higher level of social credibility and acceptance, while, to him, taking on a Creek Indian wife had more to do with securing a low but predictable flow of income and at least some wealth in the form of her allotment property than anything else. Caine didn't become rich when he married Tiger, but, through their union, he ended up with a lot more than he had before. To him, their marriage was a match made in heaven, but, for her, it was about to take off in the opposite direction.

Acquaintances and neighbors saw from the beginning that their relationship was more of a business deal for him than it was for her, but they knew she had had ulterior motives as well. Even so, it seemed clear to others that George was far more calculating than Tiger. His underlying motive was that he would become joint owner of a parcel of land that was larger than the farm he had lost money on a few years before and have access to ready flow income. Her ulterior motive was a desire for social acceptance and stability, which was much more traditional and benign than his.

A few of those who knew them argued that the prevailing outside assessment of their motives for marrying was too cynical, but it came across negatively to most people anyway, even though there was no certain way to prove the degree to which it had been a love match as opposed to a transaction. Even so, careful observation of how things went for them during the years that followed seemed to confirm that popular opinion had been right on the money.

Most of those who knew George Caine assumed that he had no higher regard for Tiger than he had for any of the Indian and black people who lived in their area, and they knew very well how he felt about them. Because his neighbors knew him to be an out-and-out bigot, why, they wondered, would he feel any different about Tiger? If he did, they thought to themselves, it would mean that a local leopard had changed his spots, and they didn't consider that very likely.

In their remote location, there were whites who considered marrying outside of their race to be beneath them. Marrying an Indian was considered less reputable than marrying within their race, but marrying a black person was codified as an illegal act. It is no overstatement to say that the Caine's lived in surroundings where certain kinds of miscegenation could lead to ostracization or, in a worst-case scenario, even to a person getting beaten or killed.

Most people in their area had no serious objection to a white man marrying an Indian; there were many of these marriages, and most of them worked out quite well. Others, however, most definitely objected to mixed marriages of any kind, and, to those who felt this way, marrying an Indian was only one step above marrying a black. They considered these marriages to be nothing more than another form of race-mixing, which they didn't approve of in the slightest.

Hoffman was but one of hundreds of towns in the south where, on many evenings, on their outskirts at some unofficial but locally well-known dividing line, hand-written signs blaring such dire warnings as "Nigger, don't let the sun set on you on this side of town" were seen on a regular basis. Warnings of this kind were justified, according to those who posted them, because similar signs using equally pointed terminology had been posted outside of some nearby colored towns, warning whites away. To certain members of both races, repeating the admonition was justified as being no more than tit for tat.   Inherited, unreasonable, pointless racial bigotry was as common in Hoffman as having a cup of coffee in the morning, since it was as isolated and as benighted as any other southern farm town.   Thinking this way was the norm, even though it made no objective sense at all.

Most of those who knew them agreed that the Colonel and Tiger's marriage was a trade-off from the get-go, in that it was probably more of a transaction of advantage to both principals than a traditional love match: He wanted property, a predictable source of additional income, and freedom to look for an easier way to make a living, while she wanted a higher social status within the community and most likely thought that marrying a white man might be a quick and easy way to take a step up in life.

Tiger saw George Caine's interest in her as being the greatest benefit of having inherited her family's allotment land and becoming the recipient of a few government allowances.   She not only understood but also found it acceptable that he was interested in her holdings, because she was convinced that he was interested in her as well.   Even if he did think of their relationship in a practical way, she reasoned, they were still legally married, and that would be enough to elevate her to where she wanted to be. She was certain that Colonel George Jackson Caine was going to be her second salvation.

— 16 —

LONG-HELD ASPIRATIONS TRUMP MARITAL OBLIGATIONS

AFTER GEORGE AND TIGER married, they moved into a comfortable home he bought for them in Hoffman proper. On top of that, he made sure the home was well-furnished and equipped with the best appliances available in local stores. It mattered very much to him that they lived in pleasant and comfortable surroundings, in the same way that it does to most everyone. Surprisingly, he did the same thing when it came to her clothing. After writing down her sizes, he went out and bought the wardrobe he wanted her to wear. He wanted—or, more accurately, *clearly expected*—his new wife to be nicely dressed.

Given her past and the way she'd been living prior to their marriage, Tiger, as could be imagined, was both pleased and impressed by what her new husband had done. Because nobody had ever paid close attention to her before, she was delighted. She didn't realize that what George had done was, well, to say the least, *unusual.*

Instead, Tiger was as pleased as punch by what her good-looking husband had done, and she was thrilled by her perceived change of status.

Convinced that he would be her ticket to the social acceptance she so very much desired, she dreamt of inviting in company, wearing her new clothes, and having all kinds of happy events in the new home he bought for them to live in as a couple.

George didn't bother to ask Tiger's opinion about any of the steps he had taken; he just went out and did them, acting entirely on his own. He didn't feel a need to tell his wife that he bought their new home by taking on a mortgage or that opened credit accounts to finance their new furniture, appliances, and clothing. Also unbeknownst to her, he had finagled a way to lease out a chunk of her—now, of course, as he saw it, *his*—allotment land as a means of raising down-payment money for the home he'd bought. He thought it was his prerogative to manage their affairs this way now that they were legally husband and wife.

Only after they were ensconced in their new home did he begin to make his expectations of her perfectly clear. It would be her role, he said, to manage what went on inside their household, while it would be his role to manage what went on outside of it, and what went on outside of it, he took care to point out, included the management of their finances.

He expected her, he said, to give their new home the best of care, to prepare good meals for them on a regular schedule, to make sure he always had cleaned and ironed clothing ready for wear, to be ready and willing whenever he wanted her, and to take care of any children they might have together. Handling these duties well, he patiently explained, was what being a dutiful wife was all about.

Earnestly promising that he would make a good living for them, he had no clue at that moment how he was going to do it. His thought was that, until he could get a handle on things, they would be able to get by on savings he still had in hand, his earnings from the barbershop, and, if necessary, by leasing out or selling off (legally or illegally) additional portions of allotment land, land that had once been *hers* but now was *theirs* but, because he was the head of their household, was really *his*. He took for granted that his ship would come before long, and that he would find a way to earn enough to pay for the standard of living he thought he deserved. Not for a second had he given up on his dream of becoming a wealthy man.

When Tiger tried to bring up a few of her own ideas about what she hoped their marriage would be like, he shushed her and said that she ought to be happy with the good things she already had. "You have a beautiful home, great furniture and appliances, new clothing to wear, good food to eat, and enough ready money to do a great job of running our household," he said. "Why," he asked, "would any woman need more than that?"

Tiger was too inarticulate and far too caught off guard by his pronouncements to say much of anything in response, but she tried to get a word in edgewise, nevertheless. That, she learned in short order, was a mistake. Persistently trying to explain her own wishes with respect to the matters she understood to be *under discussion* caused her *supposedly* devoted husband to reveal his true self for the very first time. When he did, Tiger was so surprised that all she could do was stare at him in wide-eyed amazement. Up to that moment, he had never spoken to her in anything other than what she would have described as a loving tone.

Flush with anger and without mincing words, he told her to shut the hell up and do what she was told. He was her husband, he said, and his wife was damned well going do what he said. In his household, he yelled in her face, the tail was never going to wag the dog. "In this home," he proclaimed, "things are going to be done the way I want them to be done. When I want your opinion," he said even more loudly, "I'll ask for it. Until then, you'll do what you've been told. That's how it's going to be for us, whether you like it or not, so you might as well start getting used to it!"

When, a few days later, she tried to express her displeasure by bringing the matter up again, he flew off the handle once more, this time even more angrily than before. He wasn't used to anyone talking back to him, especially not a woman and even more so not the woman who had signed on to be his lawfully wedded wife. When she refused to drop the matter, he lost his temper and slapped her around until she, as he would have put it, finally came to her senses and stopped carrying on.

Trying to reason things out with her new husband, Tiger had discovered, was never going to work. She saw in an instant that living with him was in many ways going to be just as difficult as living with her father. When she thought about what her future was going to be like, her spirit sank like a rock.

Beyond the practical activities he demanded of her, George went on to say that he expected nothing more of her than to do what she was told. How could she be the helpmate he needed, he said, if he didn't explain what help he needed? That, he explained, was all he was trying to do. More than anything else, he told her, he would not brook any behavior that interfered with what he most wanted to do in life, which was to pursue his personal and business interests as he had in the past. "I have to be all in to get where I want to be," he said, "and what that means to you is that I can't have anyone nipping at my heels over meaningless trivia while I'm out there doing my best. My gain," he continued, "will be your gain as well, so you'd better think about that before you question me again!"

What it all came down to in the end was that George had grander things in mind than Bonnie Marie Tiger, his new Creek Indian wife, and he intended to carry on in pursuit of his goals as if they had never married. He expected to go wherever he wanted, whenever he wanted, without offering a single word of explanation to her. "As long as I keep a solid roof over our heads and the heads of any children we might have together, and as long as I provide enough food for us to eat and decent clothing for us to wear," he loudly exclaimed, "that ought to be enough."

To sum up their interaction as succinctly as possible, he scared the devil out of her, in the same way as her father had, back when she was younger. Fighting back against her old man had been impossible, and she had learned that it would be equally impossible to stand up against the mighty Colonel. He couldn't have made it any clearer that he considered her personal wishes to be too insignificant and flighty to matter in the slightest.

So, at this early point in their marriage, Tiger did the only thing she could do in the wake of her husband's having come down so hard on her: She caved in, gave up, and began to behave according to the script he had described to her. In truth, it hadn't taken take too much of an effort on his part to order their domestic life the way he wanted it to be, as she was already conditioned to being used as a domestic servant and treated like a doormat.

Because her new role was so much like her old one, she fell back into it easily. It wasn't much of a jump for her to learn that her future would include having to deal with a whole lot more of what she'd had to deal with in the past. That, she bitterly concluded, must be the way men are, every miserable one of them.

After clarifying the sort of relationship he expected to have with Tiger, George went on to resume his former lifestyle. He drank when and as much as he wanted, gambled when he felt like it, and chased after any woman who was available to be chased. Because he was handsome, ambitious, and free-spirited, he caught a lot of them, too. Besides that, he had more money to spend than an average man of his day, thanks again to Tiger, and that was one more attraction he had to offer.

In all fairness, Tiger had had ulterior motives of her own before she took up with George Caine, reasons that went beyond her normal and natural human need for love and companionship, the need that caused her to put herself on display. In her case, she was in search of ordinary social approval, due to having grown sick and tired of living as an outcast. She knew George had been drawn to her as much for money and property as for herself, but that had been okay with her. She had fallen head over heels for him, that's for sure, but, as true as that was, it was also true that she thought of him as a means to an end, a way of getting where she wanted to be.

Each of them had their own motives for getting married, and the only real difference between them was that George had a clear concept of what he was doing when he did it, while she really didn't know any better. She was too naïve and unsophisticated in the ways of the world to be anywhere near as calculating as he was, nor did she have any idea where entanglement with a man like Colonel George Jackson Caine might lead. He took full advantage of her naiveté; there's no doubt about that.

The most likely direction for a connection like theirs to go after a few years of living together was straight downhill, and that, to all outward appearances, was precisely what happened. He always stayed out front, while she had to stay behind the scenes, as if she were invisible. That, it was obvious, was how he wanted things to be. Even though their relationship was viewed by those who knew them as a marriage in name only, much to everyone's surprise they stayed together for the long haul and, even after getting off to a late start, went on to have six children over the years—Walter, Carl, Ralph, Doyle, Norma, and Luther. Even so, acquaintances still doubted that Tiger and the Colonel ever enjoyed a true union of hearts and minds.

— 17 —

NOW A MONEYED MAN, THE COLONEL GETS DOWN TO BUSINESS

GEORGE CAINE WAS FAR too vain to acknowledge the impact his marriage to Tiger had on his business pursuits, but the truth of the matter was that he may not have been able to get off the ground without her. The market value of her possessions wasn't large, but she most definitely had what he was in dire need of before they got together. Co-ownership of a large tract of property, some of which was excellent lowland for farming, as well as access to Tiger's dependable stream of government payments and other allocations were more than enough to bring about a full restoration of confidence with respect to his business future. All it took to bring the real man back to the surface was knowing that he wasn't going to go under financially, at least not in the immediate future.

As quick as a flash after he and Tiger became husband and wife, George became more cocky, aggressive, and assertive than ever. Now, damn it all, he had decided, it was finally time to get after the accumulation of some real wealth. With his confidence restored by virtue of having become a mon-eyed man, his swagger returned with a great deal of gusto.

One immediate consequence of his change in status and attitude was that he was emboldened in terms of altering how he fit in down at the barbershop. Intent upon improving his earnings, he decided that he wasn't going to put up with or step aside any longer for more of lead barber Harold Upshaw's practice of hogging every damned customer who came into the business. *What kind of partnership is that?* he asked himself, paying no heed at all to the fact that the last thing most patrons of their shop wanted was for him to cut their hair. Under the circumstances, he could have cared less about catering to customer prefer-ences, nor did he care what Upshaw or any of their customers thought about anything. His only concern was himself, and what he needed at that moment was a greater share of the income brought in by the shop.

Coming on with all the subtlety of a meat axe, the overly aggressive and fully emboldened Colonel proceeded to bully and intimidate his co-leaseholder, established barber Harold Upshaw, into splitting their client base. They were co-operators of the business, insisted the Colonel, so they needed to start running it on a more equitable basis.

What "equity" meant to George was that every other customer who walked through the door of the shop needed to go to him, and that included

Upshaw's long-standing customers as well as any new ones who preferred to have Upshaw rather than the Colonel cut their hair. It would have to be explained to those who questioned their new procedure, instructed the Colonel, that this was how *they* had decided to run the shop, whether others liked it or not. He and Harold, it would have to be pointed out, both had to be able to make a living.

Upshaw, as would be imagined, was upset by the new procedure the Colonel wanted to adopt, since he saw right away what customer sharing would mean for his take. By this point, though, he had been made painfully aware of how intimidating his partner could be. The Colonel didn't convince Upshaw to accept his proposal; he bullied him into acquiescing to its terms. There's a great difference. Short of engaging in a punchout with his younger, larger, and much more aggressive partner, there wasn't much he could do about what was happening. He correctly foresaw that the new policy would have an adverse impact on his own earnings in the short run and on their shop's earnings over the long haul, but he was left with no choice but to get along by going along.

From George Caine's perspective, his agreement with his partner worked out well enough for it to become a model for many of his future business dealings in Hoffman. Strong-armed power plays may be highly questionable from a legal and ethical perspective, but they could work out very well, he had discovered, when it came to getting ahead in the business world. During the years that followed, he didn't hesitate to use similar approaches to smooth over new problems as they came up. It happened again and again, just with different people. Whatever he could get away with, he had decided, he was going to do what he needed to do to get ahead, whether others considered his efforts ethical or not. Because he was sick and tired of being poor, his approach to business dealings had become as straightforward as that.

When the new operating procedure was implemented at the shop, it worked out okay for the Colonel in the short run but not, as he had expected, over the long haul. Before long, it proved to be disadvantageous for both barbers, primarily because George was so inept at his craft. Many of those who had been repeat customers started going to nearby towns such as Dewar or Morris or Henryetta to have their hair cut, solely to avoid any chance of being routed to him. This had the effect of lowering the overall customer base of the shop and, in turn, reducing the earnings of both barbers, in exactly the way Upshaw had feared.

Before long, neither man was able to earn a decent living through their work at the shop. This was upsetting for both men, as would be imagined, but it was especially galling for Upshaw, who had been doing well for himself before George Caine arrived on the scene.

Not too long thereafter, Upshaw, ostensibly (but not actually) of his own accord, had chosen to give up his chair at the shop to take on a new job up north in Tulsa. He was afraid to publicly declare his real reason for leaving, but he told friends in confidence that it was because he couldn't stomach the thought of working another damned minute with a bully like George Caine. He hated the man, he said, but, short of getting into a knock-down, drag-out fistfight that he knew he had no chance of winning, what else could he do? He was a barber, not an obnoxious, threatening brute like the Colonel.

Through the years that followed, it wasn't uncommon for business or personal interactions between the Colonel and others to be managed in the same way that they were with Harold Upshaw. To George Caine, winning was winning, no matter how it came about. To come out on top of those who made the mistake of getting entangled with him, he didn't hesitate to use similar tactics whenever he thought he could get away with them.

Upshaw's decision to quit the shop delighted the Colonel at first, who knew that in his partner's absence he would have their whole client base to himself. Not having to split the limited number of customers who came in would mean that he finally might be able to make a decent living out the shop. That's what happened, too . . . but only for a short while.

Although he did become better at his craft after he started getting more customers and had a chance to build up more hands-on experience, George was never able to turn himself into a competent barber or muster up any decent customer service skills. Even though he put in long hours every week at the shop, his monthly income steadily declined. Before long, he got caught up in yet another ongoing struggle to make ends meet, and it finally became obvious that moving forward along the same path was just not going to work.

He ended up in the same fix as he had out on his farm: staring right in the face of yet another failure as a self-employed businessman. His situation was aggravating enough to make a grown man want to cry, and it was more than frustrating enough to make a man like George more grasping than ever. Desperation can bring that out in a person, especially one as self-focused, greedy, and unethical as the Colonel.

— 18 —

THE COLONEL STUMBLES UPON A FORMULA FOR SUCCESS

IT WAS AT THIS LATEST low point in his life that a new business concept popped into the Colonel's ever-scheming mind. Using the last of his ready cash, he took out one barber's chair and bought a pair of matching pool tables to set up at the back of the barbershop. There was plenty of room for them, especially now that he no longer had to deal with the presence of Harold Upshaw, who, the Colonel told everyone who asked, had decided on his own accord to move on for greener pastures. There really wasn't much to what he did, but it led to immediate positive results.

To encourage full use of the pool tables, he began selling under-the-counter slugs of illegal homemade whiskey and mugs of homebrewed beer to men who wanted to play a game of pool or have a few drinks while they were in town to trade, pick up mail, get a haircut, or whatever. Mr. Harmony, the owner of the shop, said he would have no objection to either move if George would agree in advance to change the name of the shop. A name change was needed, he claimed, to fully describe what his new approach to running the shop was going to be about, but his real intent was to protect himself.

Having had a few years to size up George Caine, Harmony had accurately foreseen that his leaseholder wanted to head off down a business path he had no interest in traveling. He didn't mind if Caine got on the wrong side of any high-minded residents of their community who might have a problem with the activities his leaseholder wanted to get into, but he had no interest in taking on such a risk himself. He had a reputation for upstanding behavior, and he wanted to hold on to it.

The Colonel, in the way Harmony had known he would, readily agreed to changing the name of the shop. He had known all along that Caine would love the idea of having his name prominently displayed at the front of the business. It was in this way and for this reason that "Harmony's Barbershop" became known as "Caine's Barbershop and Poolroom." This may seem to be an unusual combination of activities for a single business, but it was by no means the most unusual business name in town. For example, another business in town was named "Buchannan's Hardware, Embalming, and Picture Show." In rural settings, highly descriptive business names like these were not at all uncommon.

George Caine didn't just *like* the change of name at the shop; he was absolutely *delighted* by it, to the extent that, from that point forward, he considered the business to be *theirs*—i.e., his and Mr. Harmony's—rather than Mr. Harmony's alone, unmindful of his being only a leaseholder at the time. He didn't openly voice this thought to Harmony, but Harmony knew what he was thinking anyway. At that juncture, neither one of them had any way of foreseeing that the Colonel would remain involved in the business, in one capacity or another, for the next 33 years.

There were plenty of providers of illegal booze active in the area, men who were more than happy to secretly supply the Colonel's need for liquor at wholesale prices. So, without wasting another day, he made it known to his customers that now they could shoot a game of pool and enjoy a few drinks while they waited their turn at the shop. After that, he held his breath to see what would happen, hoping the changes he'd implement would go over as he planned, and, as it turned out, they did.

Because there wasn't much else to do in Hoffman, the new way of running his business went over well from its inception. More and more local men began to frequent the shop, mainly those who liked the idea of being able to say to their families that they were going to a barbershop rather than to a business that had, for all intents and purposes, become a saloon. The added income he earned through these new offerings didn't immediately make George a prosperous man, but he finally did start making some money out of the shop.

*****

George Caine experienced exceptional success during the years that followed, much more due to pure blind luck than to any significant level of business acumen or insightfulness on his part. The harvest he reaped from that point forward resulted much more from being in the right place at the right time than to his personal expertise. He had begun adding to his lineup of offerings in coincidence with the exploitation of oil and coal and mineral deposits that had been discovered in the area around Hoffman. It was a maximally opportune time to grow a business of the kind he wanted to run, since the combined permanent and temporary population of Hoffman and its environs jumped from around 500 to over 2,000 residents for a while, all due to the growth in business activity that was taking place.

Oil drilling and coal mining boomed in the surrounding area, and it didn't take long for workers in those fields to learn about his wide-open business. Timing and location, as always, meant everything when it came to the successful operation of a business like his, and, in this sense, George most certainly lucked out. Because he was there when it mattered, profits finally started coming in.

As men began hanging around the shop for more hours than before, the Colonel conceived of and was quick to add more attractions to keep those who were already there occupied and spending, as well as to draw new customers through his doors. Over the years, he made a series of popular changes, and, as each change was implemented, his profits continued to increase.

*****

One of the next steps the Colonel took was to partition his open-spaced barbershop so a large back room could be added, a room in which he place card tables for poker games, dominos, or checkers. Because these three activities were popular pastimes, their availability enticed men to hang around the shop for longer than they ordinarily would have, and the longer they stayed the more they drank. After he added gambling to his menu of offerings, he changed the name of the shop once again, at this point to "Caine's Barbershop and Cardroom." Mr. Harmony, because he had already taken steps to distance himself from the business, voiced no objection. He had known all along that George Caine would take off in that direction the minute he had half a chance to do so.

When the Colonel saw that men became hungry as they stayed on site for longer than they had in the past, he hired a woman who lived nearby to work evenings and on weekends making sandwiches or full dinners for men who wanted food to go along with their drinks. Lots of men, he soon discovered, wanted just that, since a good number of them were living away from their families, doing contract work for their employers. For them, having access to homemade bread or cornbread along with a pot roast or a big bowl of stew was just what the doctor ordered.

Overnight, the Colonel had come up with a whole new way of making money at the shop. Mr. Harmony was as pleased by this change as the Colonel, since George's cook bought all her commodities from his store, which was, again, only a short distance down the street from the barbershop and cardroom.

Some years thereafter, the Colonel expanded his range of offerings yet again, on this occasion by offering ice cold beer in addition to the homebrewed variety and hard liquor that had been available all along. There was no refrigeration at the time, which meant that customers who stopped by of an evening or on Friday or Saturday nights at the end of a long week of work on a farm or in a mine or on a construction site couldn't get enough of the cold beer he had to offer. He bought his ice from Mr. Harmony, who had installed an icehouse outside the back door of his general store and grocery.

Harmony bought his ice from a vendor out of Tulsa, a company that had opened a new delivery route on the highway that passed through Hoffman. Their driver used big hand-tongs to drop off whatever amount he ordered.　He opened the icehouse to serve his own customers, who loved having convenient access to fresh meat, and one of his customers was Caines's Barbershop and Cardroom.

Harmony's meat was truly fresh, too, since his slaughtering was done at the back of the store, next to his icehouse.　Hoffmanites referred to the area behind the store and beside the icehouse as a "slaughterhouse," but it was really nothing more than an outside butchering area.　Slaughtering was done for him by Chuff Crawford and Delious Allen, two local butchers who were called in as needed.　Whenever he thought there would be enough demand to sell the meat, he'd have a steer or hog butchered and hung up in the icehouse to be sold.　Fresh meat, when it was available, was advertised by a sign displayed in the front window of the store.

Harmony installed his icehouse to meet the needs of own customers, but he always ordered enough to meet the Colonel's needs as well.　Deliveries to the store were made on such a predicable schedule that all George had to do to get the ice he needed to offer cold beer and fresh meat at his cardroom was send a man a short distance down Main Street to buy it.　Having the choice of ordering cold mugs of beer as they enjoyed freshly cooked steaks or pork chops went over exceptionally well with his customers.

From the Colonel's pragmatic perspective and in his own words, *they took to it like flies on slop.*

Men ate and drank before, during, and after they played pool, poker, dominos, or checkers, and the more contented and drunker and rowdier they became, the more the Colonel and his helpers would find ways to take advantage of them. He rigged card games, used weighted dice, made use of spotters, and did anything else he could think of to extract as much money from the pockets of his customers as he could without getting caught. The Colonel had no illusions about what he was doing: He was there to make money for himself, not to look out for the welfare of his patrons. From his perspective, they damned well ought to have been looking out for themselves. To him, they were nothing more than chickens to be plucked, and pluck them he did, in every way he could think of.

*****

As the Colonel's business grew more and more freewheeling over the years, it became more well-known and popular. When it became clear that far more profit could be made from selling liquor and supplying gambling and related opportunities than from barbering or anything else, the Colonel decided to devote all his attention to activities of the more rewarding kind. He kept the barbershop, but he stopped doing any barbering himself. Instead, he subleased that part of his operation to a full-time barber by the name of Hubert "Buck" Lovett. Buck, unlike George, was truly good at his craft, and his excellent work led to even more men becoming repeat customers at the shop. His customers knew the Colonel's exit from barbering was long overdue, since he'd never been any good at it. He would never have admitted to it, but the Colonel agreed with them. He'd never really wanted to be a barber, anyway; he'd entered the profession only because, back when he first got into it, he hadn't been able to find anything else.

Using the windfall earnings that came in as years passed, he negotiated a new long-term lease arrangement with Mr. Harmony that gave him full rights over the use of the shop. On top of that, he was able to pay off the mortgage on the home he bought for himself and Tiger in Hoffman. He paid off their other debts as well, and still had money left over.

*****

With money in the bank and more free hours to work with, George was able to focus more attention than ever on expanding the more lucrative backroom side of his now thriving business. Because there were no bounds to his avarice and ambition, anything that could be done to turn a profit was alright with him. Before long, a new way of pulling even more profit out of Caine's Barbershop and Cardroom popped into mind.

Not long thereafter, two dirt paths became visible to every customer who stepped out of the back door of his business, where a month or so before there had been only one. Sooner or later, every man had to walk down one of those paths, the one that led about 30 feet to the northwest out through weeds and scrubby trees toward a highly odiferous double-seated and thin-walled outhouse that had been built for their use. The other path, which was used less often, led about 80 feet in a southwestern direction from the cardroom to a nondescript two-roomed frame building that had been hastily thrown up according to his specifications. He referred to it as his *guest room.*

In a room on the left side of the shack, behind a curtain rigged on a wire so it could easily be slid open or pulled shut as if it were a door, there was a home-made wooden double bed. The bed had a firm mattress that was covered by a few blankets and topped with a few pillows. Alongside the bed, also behind the curtain, were a nightstand, a pitcher of water, a wash basin, a stack of rags, and a coal oil lamp.

In the room at the right side of the shack close to the entry door there was a sitting area furnished with a pair of hardback rocking chairs with seats covered by homemade quilts, a cheaply made woodburning stove for use as needed, a pair of rickety end tables, and a hand-crafted coffee table. For lighting, there was a second coal oil lamp.

The Colonel had found a man he could contact as needed to have a working woman brought over from Muskogee or down from Tulsa for a single night or for several nights at a stretch. He called his contact any time he thought there would be enough business for both of them to turn a profit. When they were on hand, the provider and his female partner would eat and drink at the Cardroom as if they were ordinary customers, mainly so they could be seen by potential patrons. When there seemed to be enough interest, she would leave the cardroom and head for the guest room.

On nights when the woman was available to practice her trade, the light of the sitting room lamp could be seen through a red cloth she hung across the window beside the entryway door. If a faint red light was visible through the window, she was there for customers; when there was no light, she was not.

The new service that was available out behind Caine's Barbershop and Cardroom didn't need any advertising; word of mouth about it was more than enough. The operation was as easy to figure out as it was to use, and the beauty of the setup was that the guest room could be visited without a man having to say a word about it to anyone and without anyone but the Colonel and the couple knowing what he was up to.

"Using the number one path" quickly came to mean one thing, while "using the number two path" meant something totally different. The play on words became standing joke among patrons of the shop, and a good number of them took full and regular advantage of the discreteness with which the guest room could be accessed. The Colonel hadn't done much of anything to add this new line of service, but he still got a percentage of every dollar it brought in. With this latest addition to his menu of offerings, Caine's business became something more than an ordinary barbershop or cardroom.

There was no doubt about it: Things started to go exceptionally well for the Colonel during the years after he expanded to become the operator of a highly successful but widely considered unsavory business on Main Street, near the very center of downtown Hoffman. He knew very well that he was no more than a big fish in a miniscule pond, but that was perfectly okay with him. He was making good money, while, only a few years before, he had had no pond to swim in at all, large or small.

Another of George Caine's characteristics was that he was a man who could never get enough, no matter how much he already had in hand. Even as profits continued to roll in from his existing business activities, he never stopped searching for new ways of making even more, and he was totally unscrupulous when it came to what he was willing to do to make another dollar.

*****

Due to his innate proclivities, it was inevitable that the Colonel would get involved in activities even more nefarious than those he was into already. "In for a penny, in for a pound" was more than a slick adage to him; it was a way of life. If a particular line of business "worked"—that is, made money for him—he would work it to death, whether it was legal or ethical or not. In short order, he added two new and entirely different areas of business to his lineup of offerings, one just because he wanted to and another because it fell right into his open hands.

His first new side business was selling guns and ammunition from behind a display counter positioned at a corner of his larger operation. It was an easy add-on activity, and it was perfectly legal. He got into it simply because he had always been interested in guns and dealing with them was just something he wanted to do. His mostly male customers enjoyed looking over the limited range of high-quality rifles and handguns he stocked. Having them for sale went over quite well as a marginal sideline endeavor.

The second new sideline activity was added when, because he was known to have ready money, patrons who had financial problems began asking for loans. Why not? he decided, after thinking about it for a while, since it was true; he did have cash on hand that was not being used to turn a profit. He drifted into the loan business, in other words, only because unsolicited opportunities to do so were dropped on his lap, not due to any thoughtful planning on his part.

The problem with the kind of lending activity he engaged in was that he loaned money only at exorbitant rates and then, if anyone got behind in their payments, he did not hesitate to employ strongarm tactics to get back what was owed. Because he knew he needed to be clever about his practices, only minimal records were kept of his loans, and those that were kept were strictly off the books. Every agreement was sealed by a handshake and recorded in a notebook he kept hidden away. Every step he took was confidential.

From the Colonel's perspective, personal lending turned out to be an effortless yet highly rewarding side activity. Most borrowers paid in full when their loans were due, even when it was difficult for them to do so, mainly because it was quite clear to them from the outset that he wouldn't hesitate to be hard on them if they didn't. Collection problems did come up on occasion, but, even when they did, he didn't have to dirty his own hands to take care of them. He had a carefully developed system for dealing with that, too.

On those rare occasions when borrowers fell too far behind on a loan, he had associates to call on for help—guys he never had to ask in specific terms to do anything. This was when men like young Charley Carpenter and older but harder Walker Massey were brought into play. They were barfly hangers-on, men who, like the Colonel himself, would do most anything to avoid having to do hard work for a living. For meals and a bottle of booze on an occasional basis, they'd handle any headache Caine wanted taken care of. All he had to do was drop a hint about the problem he was having, then leave it up to them to find a way to get it solved. Getting things done through Charley and Walker was a great way of covering his tracks and keeping his own nose clean.

"Business has been lousy this month," he said aloud a day or so after a customer by the name of Joe Burley came in claiming that he wouldn't be able to pay off by the due date a loan he had taken out to buy farm implements and a freight wagon. Joe, who had a bad leg from a farm accident, went on to ask for his due date to be extended until the end of the harvest season. Joe had a bad leg that made farming more difficult for him that it was for most of his neighbors.

Making sure that Charley and Walker overheard him, the Colonel said in a disgusted tone, "I should have known better than to lend money to a gimp like Joe Burley. Now," he went on to complain, "I don't have enough on hand to pay my own damned bills this month. That's what I get," he continued, "for trying to help a sorry freeloader like him."

Both men knew very well that the Colonel had more money than he knew what to do with, but that didn't keep his concern from becoming their concern as well. They saw nothing unfair about his expecting to collect what he was owed, even on loans that were issued at exorbitant interest rates to half-desperate borrowers. That, from their perspective, was only proper. The Colonel's unyielding attitude when it came to business dealings was only one of his excellent attributes. To them, holding fast to principles of that kind was why the Colonel had achieved so much success. He had money when at a time when most other people did not, and, as far as they were concerned, that was more than enough to prove his wisdom and worth.

Charley and Walker's takeaway from the Colonel's comments that day was that until Joe Burley paid off his loan, no good luck of any kind was likely to flow downhill toward them. They knew, without his having explicitly said so, that the Colonel wanted them to find a way to make Burley pay up. They knew, too, that he didn't give a tinker's damn how they went about doing it. All he cared about was that they found some way of getting it done.

A few days later, Charley and Walker showed up early one morning at Joe Burley's rural farm, Charley with a shotgun over his shoulder and Walker with a handgun strapped to one hip. Declaring that they were on their way down to the Deep River bottom to do some hunting, Charley, smiling and friendly as he spoke, said that they had stopped for a moment to say hello and ask how things were going. Joe, of course, greeted them in kind, despite being taken aback by their having stopped by. They'd never been out his way before, and the three of them had never been any more than passing acquaintances at Caine's Barbershop and Cardroom.

Instead of standing still before Joe as the three of them talked, the two men ambled around aimlessly throughout their conversation, moving first in one direction and then in another. Before long, one of them ended up standing three or four feet to the left of Joe and the other equidistant to his right. To continue talking with them, Joe suddenly found himself having to turn first one way and then the other. Before long, his eyes began darting between them in a way that, aggravatingly to Joe, suggested furtiveness.

Within minutes, Joe got to feeling as wary as a cat. He didn't like the way his visitors were behaving, but, since they weren't doing anything that was unquestionably out of line, there wasn't much he could do or say about it. He had no idea what to make of their strange behavior. To him, everything about their visit had been weird and disorienting.

After an endless session of odd and idle chatter about first one thing and then another, Walker mentioned that he and Charley had talked for a while with the Colonel that day about the status of his various business affairs. Casually, Walker mentioned how he had complained about having not brought in enough that month to pay his bills. That, Walker said, was a problem for him and Charley, since they had done work for the Colonel that he said he couldn't pay for until he got paid himself. One of his borrowers, according to the Colonel, had not paid a bill when he was supposed to, and that had put him behind. Neither man let on that they knew who Caine was referring to, but Joe instantly realized that the Colonel had been talking about him, and that, damn it all, he thought to himself, was the very last thing he wanted to hear.

After talking their way through three or four more meaningless topics, Charley casually mentioned that they needed to get back on the road to go hunting. With that, their puzzling visit finally came to an end, and Joe was able to heave a great sigh of relief. For him, Charley and Walker's visit had been an unusual and highly disconcerting experience.

Through dinner that night and on into the late evening, Joe couldn't stop thinking about Charley and Walker's strange visit. He was still thinking about it when he went to bed, and, even after his head hit the pillow, it was still rattling around in his mind. Staring at the ceiling, he suddenly recalled a point that shook him even more: The two men had turned right when they left his farm, not left. They had headed back toward town, not down toward the Deep Fork River. That was not the direction they would have taken, he realized, if they really intended to go hunting.

Once this revelation entered his mind, Joe lay awake for the rest of the night. Now he knew for sure Charley and Walker hadn't stopped by because they were going hunting; they'd stopped by for a wholly different purpose. Who in the hell *were* they, anyway, he wondered, and *why* in hell had they really come out to his farm? He had paid no more than passing attention to either man in the past, but now that they had stood before him on his own farm, he realized that he had never seen either one doing a lick of work. *What in the world*, he asked himself, *did those two characters do to make a living?*

It was at this moment that Joe suddenly realized what their visit had been about. They were collectors, plain and simple, even though they had not said a single word about collecting. For that matter, he realized, neither had Colonel Caine, back when he asked to extend his loan. At that point, Joe felt an upset stomach coming on, and he broke out in a clammy sweat.

How in holy hell, he asked himself, *did I get myself involved with a pack of thieves like Charley Carpenter and Walker Massey and George Caine?* For that matter, what had motivated him to start hanging out at Caine's Barbershop and Cardroom in the first place? Looking back, he couldn't recall what had drawn him there. Had it been a need for association or for enough money to stay in farming another year, or a combination of both? The main thing that had become crystal clear to him was that George Caine had never been a true friend: The man was nothing short of a parasite, someone he should have stayed away from altogether, no matter what personal or financial needs he had.

Facing a mess like the one he was caught up in turned Joe into a nervous wreck. He wasn't equipped to deal with a dilemma like this, and he knew it. Realizing that there was no possibility of working things out with men like Charley or Walker or George Caine, he knew the only right choice for him was to get as far away from them as possible. Complete disentanglement from them at whatever cost, he decided, was the only way to get back to his formerly quiet and peaceful lifestyle, the kind of life he enjoyed.

When he got up in the morning, he told his wife at breakfast that he was too far in debt to be able to make ends meet on their farm. They were about to go under, he said, and it would be best for them to cut their losses rather than take on any more debt. Because his wife already knew they were in trouble, she fully agreed that he had made a good decision. Joe didn't say a word about what he owed to Colonel Caine.

After he and his wife's meeting of minds, Joe went straight into to town to have another talk with the Colonel. Upon announcing that he intended to put his farm up for immediate auction sale, he asked if he could pay off his loan as soon as it was sold. "It won't take long," he said, because he knew how quickly sales of that kind were conducted.

"Sure thing," the Colonel responded, who knew as well as Joe did that auction sales were conducted in short order. "I'm always willing to help out a friend," he said, staring directly at Joe all the while. Cringing inwardly as he listened to the Colonel's disingenuous comment, Joe saw more clearly than ever that George Caine wouldn't have hesitated to have him stomped to the ground before he'd have extended his loan, much less before he'd lose a single dollar. He didn't utter a word, though: It couldn't have been any more obvious that it wouldn't be a good time to say aloud what he was really thinking.

Joe went directly from Caine's Barbershop and Cardroom to the Hoffman Townsite and Realty Company, where he worked with one of their so-called *sole agents* to put his farm up for sale by auction. When it sold less than a month later, the first thing he did was pay off his debt to the Colonel. After that, he moved to Kansas City to live with his brother and his family until he could work out a way to get back on his feet. It would take years, he realized, to regain the ground he'd lost. That, he thought to himself, was what he deserved for having struck up a relationship with a conniver like George Caine.

A few weeks later as Charley and Walker sat at a table at Caine's Barbershop and Cardroom enjoying some good steaks, Walker had an opportunity to ask the Colonel if he'd heard how Joe Burley's farm had been auctioned for only about 75 cents on the dollar? "Yeah," Charley added, "the guy took a big hit when he sold out that way.   I'll bet it'll take him years to recoup his losses and get back to where he was."

"Well," responded the Colonel, "I didn't ask that loser to borrow any money; he asked me.   It's not my fault he couldn't pay back what he owed.   He ought to have known better than to get in as deep as he was. My guess is that he learned a valuable lesson, and my bet is that he won't be so damned dumb in the future. The only way some people learn is by gettin' their butts kicked, and Joe Burley was most definitely one of them."

Then, after enjoying a brief laugh together, Charley and Walker turned back to their steaks and George returned to tending his bar and chewing the fat with his customers.   The part they played in pushing Joe Burley into financial ruin didn't mean a thing to any of them, but to the Colonel it meant least of all.

*****

Transactions like the one with Joe Burley was only one of many such affairs the Colonel got involved in during his years as a businessman in the town of

Hoffman. He didn't win them all, but he managed to win far more head-to-head faceoffs than he lost, primarily because he was more than willing to engage in any unethical or illegal maneuver necessary to make sure he came out on top.

Underhanded and even heartless tactics enabled George Caine to be much more successful in his various business endeavors than he would have been otherwise, even to the extent of his being able to pull together enough money to buy the building in which Caine's Barbershop and Cardroom was located, the space he had leased space from Mr. Harmony. He bought it from Sil Peters, who had bought it from Harmony a while before. The building had been one of Harmony's many holdings in the town of Hoffman

The old men who served as sources for this account of the lives of George and Bonnie "Tiger" Caine seemed to recall every change of ownership of every single business that occurred over the years in the town of Hoffman. What one couldn't recall, one or more of the others did. Their collective memory was amazing, as well as captivating and enormously helpful. Without their reminiscing in tandem about old times, people, and events, it is doubtful that "The Disgrace of Colonel Caine" could have been written. To a man, one point every single contributor agreed upon was that old man Harmony had been the most admired and beloved resident of their former hometown, whereas everything any of them had to say about Colonel Caine was about as negative as it could have been.

— 19 —

AN ESTABLISHED BUT DISREPUTABLE BUSINESSMAN

IN THE WAY THAT has been described, Caine's Barbershop and Cardroom became a highly popular and financially successful watering hole in the budding town of Hoffman in Okmulgee County, out in what had once been the Indian Territory but was now the State of Oklahoma. His business became a home away from home for a good number of men, not only for temporary oil, gas, and coal field workers, but for locals as well. Nobody ever mistook it for a wholesome establishment, but it was well patronized, nevertheless.

According to those who supplied information for this narrative about his dealings at Caine's Cardroom, all kinds of arguments, fights, stabbings, and occasional killings took place there before the operation finally folded. One man was shot to death as he sat in the barber's chair, for example, doing nothing more than awaiting his turn for a haircut. Law enforcement officers and local doctors had no choice but to become highly familiar with the kinds of things that went on out there.

During the boom years of the 1920s, lots of outfits like Caine's sprang up out in the oil- and coal-belt regions of Oklahoma and Texas. Because so many patrons of these businesses were rough-and-tumble working men, it was taken for granted that all kinds of problems would crop up at them. That's certainly what happened at Caine's, not on just a few occasions but again and again.

Owners of businesses like his had no choice but to learn to think of occasional blowouts between their customers as an occupational hazard, something that came along with the turf they had chosen to inhabit. Problems of this kind were a fact of life that had to be endured, and, because they couldn't be avoided, owners had to get used to dealing with them.

The more responsible, sober-minded, virtuous residents of Hoffman were nowhere near as cavalier about the raft of headaches that were routinely spawned by the presence of businesses like Caine's. As a matter of fact, many residents cursed his outfit to high heaven, in the same way that they did all other businesses of its kind. To them, joints like his were absolute plagues against humanity, operations their town would be far better off without. Residents had become more settled than they used to be, and local leaders and prominent citizens had become a lot less tolerant of raucous goings-on than their counterparts had been in the past.

As the owner and operator of one of the previously mentioned kinds of businesses, George Caine had been able to deal with the panoply of aggravations and annoyances that were associated with running an operation like his and still manage to remain financially successful. Because he was earning good profits, he ought to have been an extremely happy man. He wasn't, though, not by a long shot, because he couldn't stop worrying about the survival of his business. It was not disputation with or between or among his customers or contempt on the part of city leaders that threatened his shady empire in the town of Hoffman. As annoying and distracting as those operating problems were, they had never been bad enough to bring him to heel. Different forces had combined to threaten his future, and one of them was his own unbridled avarice.

— 20 —

TIGER'S
WRETCHED PASSING

BONNIE MARIE (TIGER) CAINE died sooner than she should have on July 1, 1931, when she was only 48 years old. Because she was a woman who had young kids to raise, her death caught everyone flatfooted. It had never as much as occurred to anyone that such a thing could happen. The Colonel, for one, was especially upset by her demise, but not in a way that would have been described as proper for a grieving husband.

Because his various lines of business had begun to struggle due to the overall economic decline in the area and his being up to his neck in combat against his competitor Neal Easley, George Caine's first thought on the day his long-suffering wife lost her worldly battle had to do with how damned aggravating it was that it happened just when he needed her the most. As self-focused as ever, his first thought was about himself. He was too worried and preoccupied to think about how much Tiger had helped him in the past, much less about how much he was going to miss her in the future.

Officially, Tiger died of an unknown illness, but there was some conjecture at the time that she might just have grown tired of living. She might have given up, according to some of those who were familiar with her home life, due to the closeted and *on-the-shelf* kind of life she'd had to live with the Colonel. They were convinced that she had never been a truly happy person.

Her graveside service and interment at the Hoffman Cemetery were attended by her totally preoccupied husband, their six children—Walter, Carl, Ralph, Doyle, Norma, and Luther—and an assemblage of neighbors and die-hard family acquaintances. No relatives from either side of the family were present. It was a dismal, dispiriting affair, and it was presided over by a local preacher called in for the job but who knew no more about Tiger than who she was. The Caines, as would be imagined, had never been church-goers. She was laid to rest after a glib graveside presentation, which consisted of a collection of empty words that served no purpose but to add to the overall forlornness of the moment.

The only commentary that would have been fully descriptive of Tiger's life would have been to say that she ceased to exist as an ordinary human being when she became George Caine's spouse. To him, she had been more like a piece of furniture than a traditional wife, something to be used as needed and then not thought about until needed again. The man unfairly subsumed her, and she didn't deserve it. These few words would have been the only fair and truthful way of summing up Tiger's mortal experience.

George Caine's behavior toward Tiger seems to provide a vivid example of what could happen when an unscrupulous white man married an Indian woman for all the wrong reasons. Before wedding the Colonel, Tiger had recovered enough from being a domestic servant for her own father to have become a hopeful individual—a socially marginal, highly troubled, and unusual person to be sure, but nevertheless a real and hopeful person, whereas, after their marriage, she was turned into a cipher, a non-person, nothing more than a piece of property for her husband to use as he saw fit. Again, she didn't deserve it.

Why, any reasoning and fair-minded person would want to know, had she been so accepting of such appallingly unfair treatment by her husband? How did he get away with it? How was the damned guy able to turn her into his chattel, more a piece of property than an individual in her own right, and how was he able to make her, for all outward intents and purposes, cease to exist? It may seem at first blush that each of these questions would have required complicated answers, but that really wasn't so. The answers, as a matter of fact, were much less complicated than one would think.

As unacceptable and as inequitable as it may sound, Tiger responded to George's mistreatment of her as if it were something she deserved. Her behavior was more attributable to prior conditioning than anything else. For her, abuse was nothing new: She had been subjected to physical and psychological oppression her entire life. It felt to her that the Colonel had taken over where her father left off, as if he were perfectly entitled to do so. Miserable marital arrangements like hers still occur today, much less often than they used to, admittedly, but they do still happen, and they happen all over the world. In her day and context, it just happened more often, and there were fewer avenues to find a way out.

Tiger never tried to do a single thing to put an end to the way she was being treated; instead, her focus of attention was on putting up with it as best she could. She didn't think it possible to improve the quality of her daily life. Even if she had complained, it was unlikely that anyone would have stepped forward to help her. In her context, it was not particularly uncommon for a husband to abuse his wife, and what went on within a home was assumed to be no one else's business. If she had protested, the Colonel would have treated her even more harshly than before.

George's behavior throughout the years they were married made it appear for all the world that he valued her much more as a meal ticket and personal servant than as a helpmate in the Biblical sense of the term. He slapped her around whenever he considered it necessary, and his expectations of her seemed to be only that she would stay home, do as she was told, be there at his beck and call, and take care of their home and kids. Beyond that, it seemed that all he wanted from her was to leave him alone so that he could carry on in the same way he had in the past. To all outward appearances, they lived on these terms for as long as they were together.

From the beginning, their neighbors and others had been convinced that the Colonel and Tiger got together for all the wrong reasons, and that was why so many thought their marriage would be fraught with problems. How, they reasoned, could it turn out otherwise? How could things go well for them, when both partners were so unmistakably intent upon using one another as means to an end? Tiger's own relatives and acquaintances, for example, who were already estranged from her, were among those who didn't hesitate to predict that their marriage had less than a snowball's chance in hell of going well. And, as things turned out, it didn't, as the record makes perfectly clear.

There were good reasons for others to think that Tiger married George in vain hope of rising above her past and improving her station in life and that he married her only for her money, but there's no way to conclusively prove that these were their only reasons for coming together. It was at least possible that she, in her own way, did love him, and it was also possible that he, in his own way, did love her. It seems unlikely, though, due to the outwardly visible nature of their relationship, but, again, there's no way to know for sure what their life was like behind closed doors. External impressions don't always tell the full story.

Even though the Caines went on to have six children and they did indeed stay together until death did them part, there never was much outwardly convincing evidence that a loving relationship existed between them. All that could be said with certainty was that their union appeared from the outside to be just as unworkable as those who knew them thought it would be, and that Tiger was the partner who ended up holding the short end of the stick. The preponderance of evidence seemed to confirm that Tiger, as had been predicted, had gotten herself into a predicament that was way above her head. Outside observers remained convinced that, for her, marriage to the Colonel had turned out to be a clear-cut instance of jumping out of the frying pan and falling right back into the fire.

— 21 —

FAMILY LIFE UNDER
THE COLONEL'S WATCH

AFTER TIGER'S FUNERAL, George Caine and his children returned home to begin the next chapter of their lives together. He knew it would be his responsibility as the surviving parent to raise each of his and Tiger's brood of six children to adulthood, but, due to his personality and way of making a living, he dreaded the very thought of it. In view of what was going on at his business, he thought taking care of kids would be a total waste of his valuable time, and that was the last thing he could afford to do.

To those who were present for Tiger's service, it was obvious that the Colonel was going to have his hands full. They knew it would be no easy task to ride herd over a bunch of unruly kids, which was what the Caine children clearly were. It was easy to see that George and his children were going to have more problems than they knew how to shake a stick at, and not just in the future but also in the immediate here and now.

The experienced parents among those who attended the funeral knew that the totality of every scrap of knowledge George Caine had about raising kids wouldn't have filled a thimble, and it was equally apparent that he wasn't going to be up to the task. Only the worst could be expected for his children, they murmured among themselves, knowing that he was in for some very rough sledding. Even an experienced parent, they knew, would have a handful raising a bunch of pint-sized hellions as wild as his.   Nothing could be expected but for the kids and father alike to have a tough future, and, as things turned out, they were right.

Having never been much of a husband, the Colonel didn't turn out to be much of a single parent either. As others suspected, it just wasn't in his genes. After Tiger's death, he became more negligent in terms of parental duties with every day that passed, and the major reason for his negligence what that he was totally immersed in the process of keeping his business up and running. He didn't really *raise* his children, at least not in any commonly understood sense of the term; they, more accurately, raised themselves. He may have been one of the town's roughest guys, but he was an abject failure as a father.

Their mother hadn't been much better as a parent. She had done only what absolutely had to be done until each one of her kids was weaned and toddling around, and not much else after that. Because she was an indifferent and unwilling mother, she did everything she could to push her parental role into the hands of her older kids. As early in their lives as she could, she instructed them to watch out for their younger siblings, ignoring their immaturity and out-right resistance to doing what she wanted them to.

The older kids did as they were told, but they did it resentfully and on a catch-as-catch-can basis. They were kids themselves, not parents. In truth, they were worse than that: They were kids who had only a limited idea of what good parenting was all about, since they had never experienced it themselves.

George made sure to provide his children with enough to get by on, but then left them on their own after that. They came and went as they pleased and made their own decisions throughout their younger years, and lots of those decisions, as would be expected, turned out to be bad ones. They picked up all kinds of negative habits, and they were as unruly and as undisciplined as a pack of dogs.

The so-called *home* the kids lived in was never any more than a roof over their heads, a building for them to sleep in at night. Daily, they really didn't see much of their father, who rose in the morning after they had already headed off to school or elsewhere and came home late at night after they had already gone to bed. Unlike most siblings, they didn't do much to-gether, either. They saw one another in passing, but each of them went their separate ways. The kids didn't become any closer to one another than they had been to their parents. Conditions stayed this way for them for as long as they lived in their father's home. It was never *their* home; it was always *his*.

Without any semblance of effective parental supervision, it was inevitable that the children would do poorly in school, and that's exactly what happened. Every one of them dropped out before they finished the eighth grade at Hoffman Elementary School. Even those who stayed at it a while longer didn't receive a decent basic education, since they lacked even a rudimentary level of parental guidance and were therefore never serious about anything they studied.

George Caine went through the motions of parenting after Tiger died, but he had no genuine interest in watching after his kids. His kids, in turn, repaid the favor by paying even less attention to him. Except for his youngest son Luther, who admired his father's toughness, he was no role model for any of them, not in any way, shape, or form. It's tough for a local hoodlum to be a good example for his kids, even when he wishes he could, but George was one of those who didn't even wish he could. He was way too preoccupied with his own affairs to be interested. In truth, he never even thought about it.

The Caine household was nothing more to the siblings than a cold and hollow building, and it never came close to being the warm and comforting setting kids need to do well in school or in life or where any real nurturing could occur. Instead, their father's home was simply a structure for them to hang out in until they grew old enough to move on to something better.

George and Tiger were so indifferent toward their kids that none of the bonding that takes place in a normal household, the level and type of personal interaction that helps draw family members together, ever took hold in theirs. Not a one of the kids grew close to their mother before she died, nor did any of them ever grow close to their father. The kids didn't bond, either. All six of them were like ships that passed by one another in the night; they were close in terms of proximity, but they never made actual contact. Nobody in the household paid close attention to the comings and goings of any of the others. Each one did their separate things, without giving a thought to what they were missing.

With only one exception, the Caine children hung around their family home in Hoffman only until they thought they were old enough to make it on their own, whereupon they promptly flew the coop. One by one, each of them headed out for points unknown, without saying a word to anyone in advance. Each one of the kids left home when they were only in their teens, years before they were ready to do so, but, even then, they didn't think it was soon enough. The atmosphere within their home was so cold and dreary they could hardly wait to get away, and, once they left, they never looked back. Why would they, when their mother was dead and gone, their father had never played a meaningful role in their lives, and they had no relationships to speak of with any of their brothers or their sister?

Because the kids had never bonded with one another, they were children of one the biggest law-breakers in their geographical area, and Hoffman was struggling to hang on as a viable township, why on earth would any of them want to stay where they were, and why, once they got away, would they ever want to go back?   It was with these thoughts in mind that the kids, with only one exception, the youngest boy, Luther, left home as soon as they could, and, once they were gone, they stayed gone for good. They had no further contact with their hometown, their father, and no interaction to speak of with one another.

Their father, Colonel Caine, hardly knew when each of his kids departed, mainly because he was too busy with his own affairs to notice.   They were adults, as far as he was concerned, so they were en-titled to do whatever they pleased.   The bottom line for him was that he had to keep his business going, whether they stayed at home or not.

Luther was the only child the Colonel paid any attention to, and he did so in his case because it was patently obvious that the boy, unlike the others, gen-uinely looked up to him.   He considered his other kids unworthy of his attention, but he could see that his youngest son genuinely admired and wanted to emulate him. The boy's fawning attitude pleased him very much.

Because Luther was his favorite, the Colonel extended privileges to him that he did not extend to any of the others. For example, after the older children left home, he made sure the boy had parttime work whenever he wanted it. On top of that, he paid higher wages than the work he did was worth, just to make sure Luther always had some jingle in his pocket. Then, when Luther reached his teens, he went a step further by buying him a used car. It wasn't new or fancy, but having it enabled his son to stand out among his peers. He was able to go where he wanted and do what he pleased, when most other young men his age could not.

Luther, as would be imagined, was thrilled by the attention his father paid to him, since it meant that he could continue living in a way that hadn't been possible for his siblings before they left home. He took full advantage of it, too, by boozing and partying and womanizing without restraint whenever he had an opportunity to do so. It would be accurate to say that, before long, that was about all he did.

When word got back to the Colonel about his son's carousing, he was as pleased as punch about it, since he had behaved the same way back when he was a young man. His belief was that all young men needed to sow their wild oats, and, as he looked at it, the more they sowed the better off they would be as adults. From his perspective, his son was behaving in the way any red-blooded young man ought to behave, and he was proud of him. Luther was a chip off the old block, as far as he was concerned.

For many years, Luther and his father enjoyed a good life around Hoffman, but their prosperity didn't last forever. Like most other citizens of our country, they were caught off guard by the impact the Great Depression and the Dust Bowl would have on national, state, and local economies, and they most definitely didn't foresee the direct effects these events would have on the Colonel's various business activities. George did everything he could to continue running his Barbershop and Cardroom and peripheral operations as he had in the past, but it didn't take long for it to become clear that the 1930s weren't going to be anything like the two previous decades, his years of greatest success. In more ways than one, George and Luther Caine ended up being challenged like they had never been challenged before.

— 22 —

THE CURSE
OF EASLEY'S JOINT

DURING THE PUNISHING economic conditions of the 1930s and 1940s, the bane of George Caine's existence—second only to the depression itself—was a rival business he derisively referred to as "Easley's Joint," even though it was pretty much a carbon copy of Caine's Barbershop and Cardroom. It was located on the south side of town, on the east side of the road that led out of Hoffman toward Tiger Mountain and onward toward the town of Eufaula, past the curve in the road and past the railroad depot but before the bridge over the Deep Fork River. His business was marked by a faded sign with only one word on it: "Neal's." It was referred to as "Neal's Place," and it had a reputation for being every bit as unsavory as the Colonel's operation.

Some men favored one outfit over the other, but most of them patronized whichever one suited them on a given evening. Because Caine's and Easley's were the only businesses like theirs in or near Hoffman, men had to choose one place or the other when they wanted to kick back for a while. Convenience and accessibility trumped most other considerations when it came to deciding which business to visit, in the same way those considerations do when other kinds of retail, service, or entertainment businesses are selected.

In the once booming but now gradually economically declining town of Hoffman, Easley's Place most definitely was as much of a rough and rowdy honky-tonk as Caine's Barber Shop and Cardroom. The owner, Neal Easley, who had been in business a few years longer than George Caine, had already been able to build up a healthy personal estate of the kind the Colonel had long coveted. In the past, Easley's operation had never been a hindrance to Caine's Cardroom, since there had always been enough traffic for both businesses to do well. Now, though, Easley's joint had become just that, a hinderance.

Neal Easley was so well off that he no longer had to be actively involved in all the routine activities that were required to keep his business up and running. His hired man, Peter Cole, dealt with as much of that kind work for him as he could, in addition to taking care of any backhanded work he did not want to do himself. He expected Cole to help him stay as much above the fray as possible. Having Cole on hand also freed him up to come and go as needed, enabling him to deal with other business and property management activities he had under way. Both men were in and out of his primary business on a regular basis.

Just like George Caine and Neal Easley, Peter Cole was an argumentative, aggressive, contrary sort of person, a man with a well-deserved reputation for being embroiled in one hullabaloo or another nearly all the time. All three men tended to attract trouble like magnets, whether they tried to stay away from it or not. Wherever they went, it could be taken for granted that a pot of one kind or another would eventually start to boil. Easley was in most ways just like his hired man Cole, except that he had learned to be more circumspect and subtle as he dealt with problems that arose during normal business operations. Considering how the three men earned a living, there would always be something.

The men were really nothing more than lowlife criminals, the kind of guys who wouldn't hesitate to engage in bullying or intimidation or outright threats whenever they thought one of those tactics would get them where they wanted to be. Although Cole was only an employee, he was genuinely loyal to Easley, mainly because he admired how his boss had become prosperous when other businessmen of his kind had failed. Pete was Easley's man, there was no doubt about that.

Neal's business was located along one side of a dirt ball field out near the edge of town, a field that was frequently used for community-based recreation activities such as picnics and pie suppers. It was common for men to buy drinks from his bar when festivities of this kind were going on, and it had also become common for things to get out of hand at them on a regular basis. Arguments and fights flared up out on the field so often that people began to take for granted that they would happen whenever a large group got together. When men drank to excess, which they always did, it was expected that a blowout of one kind of another would occur. Flareups happened so often that they seemed inevitable. It was for this reason that local authorities and other city leaders had no more use for Neal Easley's operation than they had for George Caines's. Both businesses, in their view, were blights within the community.

Black people and whites did not comingle as social equals, but both races used the ball field and held events out there, and, when they did, they bought booze at Easley's. Over the years, Easley's place and the area around the nearby playing field had become as notable as Caine's Barbershop and Cardroom for being a top site in Hoffman for drunken revelries, arguments, fights, stabbings, and occasional murders. When it came to problems of this kind, Easley and the Colonel ran businesses that were alike in every respect but their names.

Selling homemade beer and liquor under the counter was a widespread practice throughout the region. Illegal whiskey bottled in jars or jugs was sold not only by the two leading bar owners but also by most of the town's otherwise respectable retail dry goods and grocery establishments, just on a more limited scale. Business owners who would have preferred to operate fully on the up and up often looked the other way when it came to this one product, knowing that they had to, if they wanted to remain competitive. Seedier establishments, of course, like Caine's and Easley's, had no reservations about selling every drop of alcohol traffic would bear.

Games of chance, notably throwing dice and playing card games, went on every weekend at the town's only two dives. Gambling and betting were so popular that even the town jail also became the site of regular weekend throwdowns. Prisoners who could afford to do so could shoot dice on the ground by slinging them through the bars on the front door of their temporary abode. Gambling at this location occurred on a routine basis, with prisoners happily taking on anyone who was willing to come by with a bottle and keep them company for a while. One regular visitor at the jail was local Pentecostal Preacher Jack Daniel Parker, who dropped by whenever he could to drink and play, always justifying his participation by claiming that it was the best opportunity he had to reach out to and possibly reform some of the town's most unrepentant troublemakers.

It was rumored that on some Sunday evenings, Parker would go straight from the church to the jail to mingle with any man or men who happened to be locked up. He played cards and shot dice, he said, because it was his only means of making real contact with men of their kind. "If I don't have a way to interact with them," he asked, "how can they ever be converted?" His was an unusual approach to evangelism, even for a backwoods town like Hoffman.

It was suspected (but never proven) that, when no one was looking, Parker took money out of his church's collection plate to spend on liquor and gambling. There was no lack of controversy about the propriety of what he was doing, but no one ever stepped forward to challenge him. Everybody liked Jack Daniel Parker, not just because he was exceptionally charming and personable but also because he shepherded a successful and effective church and was thought to be an excellent preacher. His congregation was prospering, so there was never sufficient incentive for anyone to rock the boat by openly accusing him of wrongdoing. On top of that, it was indisputable that some of the more hardcore miscreants of the community really did occasionally turn up at church on Sunday mornings, proclaiming that they were there to hear Preacher Parker. "There isn't another preacher in town," Parker could boast, "who can claim that kind of success!"

What made George Caine and Neal Easley so much alike was that they had accumulated their wealth through pandering to every weakness in their fellow men they could detect and somehow coming up with a way to work it to their advantage. Any vice that could be exploited was equally acceptable, no matter how unsavory or harmful.

If money could be made through manipulating weaknesses or unhealthy habits, that was all they needed to know. If their customers wanted alcohol, they'd stock any kind they asked for; if they wanted to gamble, they'd stoke up any game that was in demand; if they wanted tobacco, they would get whatever form of it anyone desired; and if they wanted access to women, they'd have some brought in out of Tulsa or Muskogee. When it came to meeting their illicit wants, Caine and Easley really did think their customers were always right.

Ordinary tobacco products were a steady source of income for both men, in the same way that they were for every other business in town that carried them. Consumed through smoking, chewing, or dipping, the leaf was widely used, even more so than it is today. "Back then," one source of information for this story asserted, "big old spittoons was sittin' around everwhere you looked, and the floors in some bars and outhouses was so slick with brown juice they was nasty as hell. Women done it too, some of 'em, by gosh, worse'n the men. People couldn't do without their tobacco, so they went around dippin' snuff or chewin' and spittin' or smokin' that damned stuff everwhere you looked."

Through actively capitalizing on any vice that could be harnessed as a means of making money, Colonel George Caine and Neal Easley had built up profitable businesses in the town of Hoffman. In the process, they built up notorious local reputations as well. They were known as the go-to guys for anyone who wanted a little high life or illicit action of any kind. It had also become known that getting crosswise with either one of them was inadvisable, since on numerous occasions both had shown a willingness to do whatever had to be done to make sure involvements went the way they wanted them to.

Easley was also like George Caine in being highly pleased with himself for having been able to accumulate a good deal of wealth over the years, and he didn't hesitate to blow his own horn when there was an opportunity to do so. He was known within the community for boasting about how well he'd done. There was nothing shy about Neal Easley, and personal vanity was only one of several traits he and George Caine had in common. In this area, the two men were like matching mules in trace.

Colonel George Caine's unspoken goal, as a matter of fact, was to get to the point where he could be as proud and boastful as Neal Easley already was. If the truth could have been told about them, that's what would have been said. Without a doubt, jealously and envy were two of the Colonel's vexing green-eyed monsters.

The over-arching problem Caine and Easley had in common was that the economic parameters within which they operated their businesses had been altered. They couldn't change the fact that there no longer was enough of their kind of business for both of their enterprises to do well in Hoffman, and, as the local economy continued to head further south, peaceful coexistence between them was no longer an option. It was do or die time for both men, whether they wanted it to be that way or not. It was obvious that something was going to have to give, but each man adamantly swore that he wasn't about to do any giving.

The Colonel's major problem was that his business had grown so popular that it was drawing too many customers away from Easley's operation, and Neal Easley couldn't stand it. Their businesses had coexisted fairly well during the economic upswings of the 1910s and '20s, but it had become apparent to both men that those good times were over. It had become clear to anyone who was paying attention—and George Caine and Neal Easley were paying much closer attention than anyone else—that if things stayed as they were, one or the other of them would go broke, and it was this fact that led to the third of the Colonel's three business failures in the town of Hoffman.

Through their use of questionable business practices and various other underhanded activities, Caine and Easley had become sufficiently well off that, by any reasonable standard, they ought to have been happy men. They were not, though, neither one of them. Both men suffered from an identical affliction, which was that each was galled by the other man's success. Jealous and envious in the extreme, they had become obsessed with each other, even to the extent of lying awake at night, wondering how in holy hell they were going to deal with the one great problem they had in common, which was how to go about doing their competitor in.

Each man bitterly resented and envied any success the other man was lucky or astute enough to achieve. Things had reached a boiling point, now that competition between them had become ruinous and their means of earning a living were clearly under threat.

Night and day, both men worried about how they were going to keep their business up and running and profitable. They had grated against each other for so long that all either one of them was able to think about was the other man's presence. For years, relations between them had been strained but endurable, but of late their relationship had become so frayed that they could hardly stand the sight of one another. It was clear that even something as incidental as passing each other on the street, which was impossible not to do in a town as small as Hoffman, might lead to a spitting match or something even worse. Due to the severity of the economic decline, there was too little of the kinds of activities their businesses depended on to meet the needs these two avaricious competitors.

Caine and Easley knew all about one another from a distance, but their relationship was no deeper than that. Through customers and other contacts, each one heard daily comment about what the other man was up to. They avoided each other whenever possible, to the extent that they crossed paths only by accident. Even so, now that their livelihoods were unmistakably on the line, they had become as jealous and resentful of each other as it was possible for them to be. Because they were equally un-scrupulous schemers and connivers, they hated each other with a vengeance. Nobody had to tell them that their economic futures were at stake; they knew it better than anyone. For both men, the other had become an ever-present thorn in the flesh

Every resident of Hoffman knew that bad blood existed between the Colonel and Easley, since for years both men had been bitterly and vociferously maligning each other within their inner circles, making no secret of their animosity toward the other. It was abundantly clear that tempers were about to boil over, now that both men had pulled out all the stops and begun verbalizing in public the scathing comments they usually said in private. Openly bad-mouthing another man was not done in a location like theirs, not unless the man with the big mouth was ready and willing to fight over what he had to say. They were senior men who ought to have known better, but they were so locked in on their views that common sense no longer mattered.

"Things was about ready to get out of hand between them two gangsters," one old-timer recalled, "and everbody damned well know'd it. Everbody was as happy as hell about it, too, hopin' they'd kill one another. Everybody know'd Hoffman would be a hell of a lot better off if they did!"

One of the seniors who provided information for this story said that his father, who was a teacher at Hoffman School when Caine and Easley's quarrel took place, had told him all he knew about it. "My father made an excellent point in saying that talking about their argument years after the fact somehow minimizes the significance of what took place between them. Today, their conflict comes across as being easily avoidable and almost laughable. Looking at it that way is wrong, though, considering the devastating effect the outcome of their conflict had on our town. Today, it sounds like a hackneyed or throw-away event, but it was as serious as all get out to everyone who lived there at the time. It wasn't something you could dismiss and ignore, not if you wanted to make a living in Hoffman!"

To Caine or Easley or to anyone else who was around when their affair was about to come to a head, there was nothing humorous about what was sure to happen. It had become as clear as a bell that a full-fledged battle between the two men could break out upon the slightest provocation. "If push does come to shove," one local man was said to have exclaimed, "you can bet your ass that Pete Cole's gonna be at the very center of it. You can mark my words on that!" He was only guessing, of course: There was no way anyone could know at the time how things were going to play out, and, in the end, the fellow's guess turned out to be no more than rank speculation. Later, after the conflagration was all said and done, it was discovered that Cole played no part in it at all.

— 23 —

A CLASH OF
LOCAL HEAVYWEIGHTS!

JOHN DAVID HARMONY'S General Merchandise and Grocery Store was the hub of the local retail and grocery trade in Hoffman.   His well thought-of establishment was located on the west side of Main Street, just over one block north of the intersection of Main and Broadway, which was the geographical center of town, and about one block from the building on the same side of Main that had once been Harmony's Barbershop but was now Caine's Barbershop and Cardroom.   Both businesses were in sight of the community water well, which was located at the southeast corner of the intersection of Main and Broadway. Neal's Easley's business was less than a mile further south on the east side of Main, out past the railroad depot and the curve in the road but before the bridge over the Deep Fork River.   It was not visible from Caine's or Harmony's.

There were a few other grocery and dry goods stores in Hoffman, but most local people did their trading at Harmony's. Colonel Caine and Neal Easley, for example, were among his regular customers.   Harmony's Store drew in customers for a host of reasons that went beyond the good line of dry good and groceries he carried, and three of those reasons were as straightforward as they could be.

The major reason Harmony's Grocery and Dry Goods operation was so well patronized was its proximity to the Hoffman Post Office, which was situated in a separate space at the southwest corner of the same commercial building that housed his store. Because the door into the post office was only a short walk away from the entryway of the store, lots of people got in the habit of going into Harmony's after picking up their mail. Why not, they figured, when it was so convenient to do so. Then, because they were already there, they went on to do at least some part of their regular trading while they were on site. Some of them, in fact, did all their trading there, so they would not have to make another stop.

Neighbors interacted with one another as they picked up their mail and did whatever trading they had to do, and when they talked it wasn't uncommon for them to chatter like magpies. Unexpectedly passing by a neighbor in a town like theirs often took on greater significance than it did in larger cities, due to their not seeing one another all that often. Simple occasions of this kind were treated as great opportunities for people to visit and catch up on all sorts of things. In fact, these interactions often became more like mini social events or special occasions than casual passing conversations. In communities populated mostly by hardworking farmers, that's how things tend to be.

Those who live in farm communities like Hoffman rarely got in much of a hurry when they met up, since living in isolated rural areas creates a pressing need for people to talk, visit, and stay connected. Whether they would have admitted to it or not, many such people welcomed any opportunity that came up to interact with their neighbors. This is a predictable aspect of existence in rural towns everywhere, wherever they are located.

Mr. Harmony had done everything he could think of to keep people in his store for as long as possible, since the longer they stayed around the more they tended to spend. Summer and winter alike, neighbors visited and talked with one another while they were there, often as they sat on chairs that had been positioned at a back corner of the store or on benches that had been set out front.

A second major drawing card Mr. Harmony had made available was a big pot-bellied stove around which his inside chairs were circled. For male and female customers alike, the corner had become one of the most popular stop-offs in town. It was a setting in which neighbors could touch bases with neighbors in comfort, and it had become unthinkable for anyone to go to town without ducking in for a while. Many dropped in for no other reason than to look for bargains among the personal ads Harmony allowed customers to post on the wall behind the stove. "Everbody wanted to see them ads up on that wall," one source said. "More often than not, the stuff that was up there wasn't worth nothin', but ever once in a while you could find some stuff worth buyin'."

A third major reason why Mr. Harmony's store became so well patronized was the icehouse he installed in the 1920s, the one Colonel Caine came to rely on so heavily for his business. Tulsa had an electrical power plant, but most rural towns in Oklahoma—towns such as Hoffman—were not electrified until the late 1930s. Even after residents got electrical power in their homes in later years, they remembered how much they appreciated Mr. Harmony's having added that icehouse. It created goodwill that lasted for the next couple of decades.

The icehouse was located a few steps outside the back door of his store, in a thick-walled natural rock room that had been constructed for this purpose and affixed to the back of the building. It had two doors, one that opened to the outside behind the store and one that opened into the store itself. The inside door opened into the store proper, right into the work area behind the main counter. The icehouse and the space behind the counter were connected by means of a pull-down slide rail that was equipped with a dangling meat hook. All Harmony's counter clerks had to do to display whatever fresh meat he had for sale was open the back door of the icehouse, then pull in slabs of meat hanging on the hook along the rail and into the store. Getting meat from the icehouse and making it visible to potential customers took no more than a few minutes.

Access to fresh pork or beef on a regular basis had become a major drawing card for Harmony's business. People had no reliable means of storing meat at home, since refrigeration had not yet become available. Customers knew Harmony's meat was fresh because they knew his clerks cut it from livestock slaughtered behind the store, right beside his icehouse. They also knew his butchers, Chuff Crawford and Delious Allen, as well as where his slaughter stock came from. When fresh meat was available, they knew that there would be a sign saying so in the front window of the store.

It was abundantly evident to patrons why Harmony made these innovations and comforts available, but they appreciated his thought-fulness anyway. They knew, just as he did, that their best option was to deal with his store, whether he offered any special comforts or not. Everyone in town had high regard for Mr. Harmony's business acumen, but they valued him as a friend as well. He was personally acquainted with every one of them.

J. D. Harmony knew how to build a clientele, there was no doubt about that. There were good reasons for his having become one of the most successful and most revered of the town's legitimate businessmen. Even so, several of the elderly former residents who served as sources for this account of Colonel Caine's exploits in Hoffman couldn't restrain themselves from pointing out that even though Harmony was universally considered a highly ethical and admirable merchant, his reputation had not stopped him from making extra money by selling supplies to questionable operations such as Caine's Barbershop and Cardroom and Easley's Bar. In addition, he also carried all the supplies and furnishings required by local men who made illegal whiskey and home brew, and extended credit to them as needed.

"He'd buy their finished stuff, too," one of the men said, "and then sell off at under-the-counter prices out of his store whatever he did not sell to Caine or Easley, since some bootleggers preferred not to get involved in direct deals with either one of them two. Lots of them store owners done the same thing as Harmony," he confided. "That's how some of 'um got as blasted rich as they was!"

Be that as it may, everyone took for granted that, before long, Caine and Easley were going to clash, since their feud had simmered for so long that their tempers were near the boiling point. It was no longer a matter of *if*, people said; it was only a matter of *when*. In a town the size of Hoffman, it was bound to happen. It was impossible for them to avoid each other forever.

It was also taken for granted that, when the men did bump into one another, it would happen at one or the other of the locations in town everyone sooner or later visited: Harmony's Store or the space at the southeast corner of the building in which his store was located, the room that housed the Hoffman Post Office. People kept their eyes wide open when they saw either man near the building, hoping that the other would turn up there as well. Their crossing of paths was eagerly anticipated.

Cautious citizens quietly stepped away when either man was around, but those who were bolder stayed close and kept on the alert in case anything came up. Because a conflagration was inevitable, those who were more adventurous wanted to be on hand when the fat hit the pan, knowing that any interaction that took place might end quickly. It was rare for anything momentous to happen in Hoffman, so they wanted to be around if it did.

*****

The conflict between Caine and Easley came to a head on August 5, 1943, when they bumped into each other at one of the locations where most everyone thought they might—at the front counter of J. D. Harmony's Dry Goods and Grocery Store. The clash of the local heavyweights was finally at hand.

The two thugs got into the vicious argument that everyone expected, but not a single resident of Hoffman was prepared for what happened from that point forward. Their engagement ended in a more awful way than any one in town, including the primary combatants, could ever have imagined.

What everyone anticipated—and, for that matter, longed to see—was an actual physical altercation or gun battle between the well-known tough guys, a fight that would leave one or the other or, even better, both lying out in the street, as dead as bricks. If that were to happen, they figured, their town would be a lot better off.

That, though, was far and away from how the conflict between the principal antagonists worked out. What happened instead was that the town of Hoffman ended up losing one of its most venerated, most successful, most influential, and most beloved citizens, merchant J. D. Harmony. When residents heard this, it seemed impossible that such a thing could have happened, but it had. And, as if to add insult to injury, it had happened as a side effect of the longstanding bitter feud that was going on between their town's most notorious citizens, George Caine and Neal Easley.

Of all people, the praiseworthy J. D. Harmony was the only one who died that fateful day, and that's why the outcome of a fight that was supposed to have been between Caine and Easley sent shock waves throughout the community. It also explains why so many residents remembered the fight between these hoodlums for so many years thereafter. Most of the town's reputable citizens were disappointed that neither one of the lowlife antagonists whose feud brought about the conflict had suffered as much as a single scratch.   How on earth, people asked in wonderment, could such an awful outcome have come to pass?

— 24 —

HOFFMAN TOWNSITE SUFFERS A CRIPPLING BLOW

BECAUSE EVERY MAN who was present offered up a slightly different version of what transpired on the day Colonel George Caine and Neal Easley butted heads at J. D. Harmony's Dry Goods and Grocery Store, it took a lot of time and effort to reconcile the differences between their disparate accounts. Eventually, though, it was possible to put together a coherent, generally accurate composite of what happened on that tragic occasion.

The conflagration between the Caine and Easley got started in a totally unexpected way, not in consequence of a direct argument between them but due to their becoming involved in a shoving match that had broken out between Tom Shipley and, of all people, Preacher Jack Daniel Parker. It was the last thing anybody expected, but that's how it got underway, nevertheless; every witness agreed on that.

It happened when Shipley was on duty as one of the counter clerks who worked a rotating shift for Mr. Harmony and Parker came into the store as a customer. Jack Daniel—or *Preacher Parker*," as he was called—was, as mentioned earlier, pastor of the local

Pentecostal Holiness Church. Some Hoffmanites brushed him off as a pretender, but others considered him to be a genuine hellfire and brimstone man of God—a preacher who, as one witness put it, "know'd his Bible backwards and forwards."

Whether he was genuine or not, one point widely agreed upon was that Preacher Parker had a history of getting himself involved in one theological controversy after another in their community, and, when he did, he was known for never backing down. He had always been stubborn, even as a boy.

Like many self-educated preachers, Parker wasn't much different from most of his flock in terms of fundamental beliefs, but he was a world apart from them in terms of temperament. He was a man with rough edges, and he didn't hesitate to share his opinion when he thought he was right about something. This was especially true, according to those who supplied information for this story, when it came to scriptural matters that were near and dear to his heart. As one source put it, "Jack Daniel could be way too outspoken, and he was as bullheaded as a mule. He was a mean son of a buck when he was a kid, but, later on, after he got older, he got real religious. That was when he started preachin' for the Holiness Church."

Others added that Parker was well known for his tendency to become overly assertive and aggressively zealous when it came to his religious convictions and for having an irritating tendency to push his opinions harder than most people could stomach. Those who had become butts of his barbs and critiques hadn't always taken them well. In addition, a good many people felt that some of his clerical practices had never been particularly preacherlike. Shooting dice and playing poker down at the jail using collection plate money, for example, was one practice many had no sympathy for, and there were other bones of contention against him as well.

One additional problem for Parker, for example, was that he had epilepsy, and he had it in a setting where few people understood the affliction. Occasional and unexpected seizures added yet another concern to his already suspect local standing.

Tom Shipley, who was an ex-farmer, was not the most customer–oriented of Mr. Harmony's counter clerks, in that he was a tall and lean and gruff sort of man. He lived over by Hoffman School, only four blocks away from the store. People considered him something of a grumpy old SOB, partly because he lived alone in the old T. C. Varner house but mainly because he had some unusual beliefs and routinely engaged in practices that were thought to be quite strange. If someone suffered a cut, for example, he would read a verse out of the Bible to help stop the bleeding. Some young boys in town were afraid of him due to his grouchy disposition, but most people just dismissed him as being mean, cranky, and weird.

Before Colonel Caine and Neal Easley met up that day, Preacher Parker and Tom Shipley had somehow managed to get into an argument at the front counter of the store, an argument that had suddenly gotten loud and gone public. Most sources agreed that it started when the preacher criticized Shipley's misuse of Biblical scriptures, and, since there was too much agreement among the witnesses for this take on the cause of their argument to be wrong, there's no doubt that that's exactly what happened.

Shipley and Parker were well known to have argumentative dispositions and tempers to match, and words had been exchanged that caused a bitter exchange to break out between them. In a flash, it had evolved first into a shouting match, then to various threats, and finally into an exchange of pushing and shoving. The whole thing broke out so suddenly that everyone in the store was caught off guard. Those who described their quarrel afterwards didn't hesitate to say that it was caused by "Preacher Parker's smart mouth" and because "he never did know when to back off."

When Parker popped off about some of Shipley's personal religious convictions that he had no right to comment on, question, or criticize in any way, Shipley lost his temper and told him to mind his own damned business. Their interaction spontaneously and unexpectedly took a turn for the worse when the slicker-tongued preacher got so far under Tom's skin that he couldn't take it anymore. Feeling bested by the preacher's glib wording, Tom impulsively decided to fight back with his fists. That's when their shoving match began, and immediately after that it turned into an ugly argument.

Most of those who were on hand that day—whites, blacks, and Indians alike—were so stunned that a blowout had broken out between Parker and Shipley that it didn't immediately occur to any of them that someone ought to step forward and try to break it up. Everyone just stood there, hanging back quietly but listening intently, taken aback by what was happening. They weren't surprised to hear the men arguing, but they were most certainly amazed that a physical confrontation had broken out between a store clerk and a Pentecostal preacher. To repeat a comment one man's father said he overheard at the time, "You sure as hell don't see that ever day!"

As it happened, the Colonel was among those present when the argument between Parker and Shipley got out of hand, but the difference between him and the other observers was that he was accustomed to seeing arguments of the kind that was taking place. Because that sort of thing was a common occurrence at his cardroom, their blowout didn't disturb him in the least.

He, unlike the others, began egging Parker and Shipley on, eagerly hoping that they'd get in a down and dirty fistfight. "There wasn't nothin' Caine would of liked better than to see Parker get busted up," some said for the record. "Everbody know'd Caine never liked any of the preachers in town, mainly because he know'd they talked about him when they preached. None of them liked the Colonel, and the Colonel sure as hell didn't like none of them. Most of all, he didn't like Parker, because he'd heard that Parker raised hell about him nearly ever Sunday! It was true, too."

Then, just as the argument between Shipley and Parker was reaching a peak and they were about ready to go to blows, Neal Easley walked into the store. For a minute or so, Easley and the Colonel were no more than fellow spectators of somebody else's argument, just like everyone else who was present that day. "When I was young," said one source, "there was a lot of guys who'd run *to* a fight, not *away from* one, as long as they wasn't in it themselves."

Things changed for the worse in a heartbeat as soon as Caine and Easley became aware of each other's presence. Easley, it was said, chose to take great offense at Caine's egging on Shipley and Parker to fight, but accordin' to some of those who were there "if Caine hadn't of been doin' the eggin' on Easley would have been doin' it himself. When it came to arguments, he was just like the Colonel; he didn't like nothin' better that a good fistfight. There's no doubt about it, though; it was what Caine said and done after that that really tore things loose."

"That's true," said another man who had heard all about the event, "My father was there in person that day, and he said that the Colonel was a man who always had somethin' smart-assed and aggravatin' to say about everthing that ever happened, even about an argument that didn't have nothin' to do with him. He didn't have no right to get between Jack Daniel and Tom Shipley like he did, but he done it anyhow, and that made Jack and Tom mad enough to spit nails. When he kept goadin' them to go on and fight, both of 'em suddenly turned around and started cussin' him out, saying that he ought to butt out and mind his own damned business.

Well, when Parker and Shipley both started tellin' the Colonel he ought to butt out, that's when Neal Easley couldn't resist shootin' off his mouth, too. Everybody know'd he was just usin' what was happin' as an opportunity to tear into Caine. He'd been lookin' for a chance to start somethin' with him, and he decided that Shipley and Parker's argument would be a wonderful opportunity to do it.

'Yeah,' Easley said, 'this whole damned town would be a lot better off, Caine, if you stayed the hell out of everbody's business.' He was really thinkin' about his own business, of course, rather than suddenly becomin' civic minded, but in the heat of the moment nobody picked up on it. To Easley, because he got started in Hoffman first, George Caine wasn't nothin' but an interloper, even though he'd run a business in Hoffman for the past 30 years.

Well, as soon as Easley made that smart-assed remark to the Colonel, the argument between Parker and Shipley was forgot as fast as you can kick a cat. Everbody know'd they were about to see a real fight instead of a hissing match between a preacher and a local crackpot, and it was one they'd been waitin' on for years. You don't cuss a man in public, not unless you're willin' to back it up!

Before anybody had a chance to size up what was happin', Easley and the Colonel was squared off and gettin' ready to get after it, in the way everbody know'd they was goin' to all along. It looked like things between them was about to get settled, once and for all!

Just then, though, Mr. Harmony, who'd decided he'd heard enough arguin' and fightin' in his store, ran out of his back office and charged out in amongst all the men that was arguing and everbody else that was standin' around, yelling for the whole damned bunch of them to get the hell out of his store. 'I don't give a damn if you knock each other's brains out,' he yelled; 'just get your sorry asses out of my business before you do it!'

My dad said that J. D. Harmony didn't get mad often, but, when he did, he could be as mean of a son-ofabitch as anybody else. He didn't get where he was by bein' afraid of a fight, that's for damned sure. Everbody know'd he kept a pistol an' a shotgun behind the counter of his store, just in case anybody ever took a notion to rob him. Nobody ever thought he was afraid to use it, either!

Anyhow, just as Mr. Harmony jumped into the midst of all of them fools to keep 'um from beatin' on one another to death in his store, Tom Shipley suddenly broke away from the group, ran behind the counter, and grabbed the pistol Harmony kept on a shelf below the cash register. He kept it there, like I said, in case he ever got robbed, and nobody ever thought a thing about it. Nobody with any sense would want to be surprised by a thief, no more than Mr. Harmony did.

Shipley said he went after the gun to run everybody out of the store, thinking that that was what Mr. Harmony wanted. Mr. Harmony, he said, wanted everybody who was arguing run out of the store, and I worked for Mr. Harmony, so, damn it all, that's exactly what I intended to do. I had no intentions of shootin' anybody!

Everbody was as surprised as all get out when at that point the Colonel suddenly lunged forward to grab the gun away from Tom Shipley, tryin' to tear it out of his hand so's he could use it to kill Neal Easley. Everbody know'd that was exactly what Caine wanted to do, even though he denied it all to hell later on.

'That damned well wasn't what I was gonna do,' the Colonel said. 'All I wanted to do was keep anybody from gettin' hurt,' he claimed, but nobody believed a word of it.

What everbody thought," Shipley continued, "was that the Colonel had gotten so cockeyed mad at Easley that he went off the deep end for a while. Everbody thought he woulda killed him if he could. That, though, was only what everbody thought. There never was no way to prove it."

"Anyway," another onlooker recalled, "what happened next was that Mr. Harmony lunged that way too, trying to get ahold of the gun hisself, knowin' damned well what the Colonel would do if he got his hands on it first.   As crazy mad as the Colonel was at Easley, Mr. Harmony saw as quick as a wink that the Colonel would kill him if he got a chance.   Everbody, not just Mr. Harmony, knew he was mad enough to do it, too. So did Neal Easley. Before anybody know'd what was happin', those five men as well as some of the bystanders was fightin' and pushin' and cussin' one another at the same time, all of them strugglin' either to get control of that gun or pull people off one another."

It was in this clumsy way, according to the composite eyewitness accounts, that things got far enough out of control for an incident that would have amounted to no more than one smalltown bully beating up or shooting another smalltown bully to turn into a tragic incident that affected the entire town of Hoffman.   What happened was that although

Mr. Harmony was able to keep the Colonel from getting control of the gun, he was not able to keep it from discharging. When it did, the track of the bullet was deflected downwards, directly into his own left leg.

The bullet struck J. D. Harmony between the knee and the hip, causing him to scream in pain and fall to the floor with a thud. When blood began pouring out of his wound in a torrent, all hostilities ceased in a heartbeat. Except for Mr. Harmony's moaning, the store became as quiet as a church. Everyone could see that he was very badly hurt.

This, everyone recognized in an instant, was an outcome more inconceivable and unexpected than anybody at the melee would have imagined in a million years. Their town's most affable, most beloved, and most successful citizen, the venerable merchant J. D. Harmony, had been shot, and now, there he was, lying prostrate on the floor and writhing in pain, right before their eyes. After looking at him closely, everyone saw that he was gasping for breath and bleeding profusely, and it appeared for all the world as if he were about to die.

For a moment, every one of the men could do no more than stand there, staring down at Mr. Harmony, shocked into silence by the sight before their eyes. It took a while for some of them to come to their senses, but, once they did, they saw that Harmony's wound was indeed life-threateningly severe. Working together, several of them lifted him from the floor and carried him in their arms out of the store, down the front steps, and over to where one of the bystanders, a Creek Indian by the name of Will Phillips, had pulled up his car to receive him.

As soon they got Mr. Harmony into the back seat and in a position that was as comfortable as possible under the circumstances, Phillips and a carload of men sped off to take him to be treated by Dr. G. Y. McKinney at the Haynes Hospital, which was eight miles away over in Henryetta. A train of other cars followed along behind them, each one carrying a load of bystanders or residents who had heard about what happened, all of them worried sick over what might become of their good friend and leading citizen, J. D. Harmony.

Those present were so agitated by what had happened that they drove off and left the store as well as the cash register drawer wide open, making their contents accessible to anyone who happened to walk by. Nobody, though, as it turned out, ever touched a thing. "Everbody," according to the record, "respected and cared that much about Mr. Harmony. Many of them had know'd him all their lives. Lord, it was more like somebody's own father or a mayor or a governor had been shot than a local businessman. People were shaken all to hell by it. Harmony wasn't no ordinary storekeeper; he was a cornerstone of our whole town!"

Tragically, the bullet from his own gun had hit a major artery in Harmony's left leg. Twisting and moaning in excruciating pain and bleeding copiously while wedged between men supporting him in the back seat as the car roared toward the hospital in Henryetta, he bled to death before they could get him there. There was no opportunity to attempt to revive him. He was dead when they arrived at the door of the building, sprawled out over the legs of men who had been his customers, neighbors, and personal friends.

After a funeral service five days later that was officiated by Reverend C. A. Spillers and Chaplain John D. Seals of the McAlester State Penitentiary that was attended by most everyone in Hoffman, Mr. Harmony was interred in a family cemetery close to town. His obituary was written up in the Eufaula Indian Journal and other area newspapers. The day of the funeral was highly unsettling for everyone present, not only because Mr. Harmony was dead, which was bad enough in and of itself, but because it was becoming clearer than ever that his death was going to be as much of a terrible blow for Hoffman as a civic entity as it had been for his family.

In the weeks and months after the shooting, residents had a great deal of difficulty coming to grips with the fate that had befallen their town. Everyone felt disoriented and at loose ends. The more people thought about what had happened, the more personally offended they became. J. D. Harmony had been one of their most prominent, revered, and conscientious citizens, a man who was known and esteemed by everyone. Now, here all of them were, without one of their most exceptional community leaders, and he was gone only because he had tried to break up an argument between two of their area's shadiest residents. "How," people asked themselves, "could such an awful thing have happened?"

After giving the matter a lot of serious thought, most people concluded that the shooting was an event that shouldn't be categorized and then dismissed as a tragic accident that ought to be forgotten. They didn't think it ought to be forgiven, either, since it was too much of a civic body blow for an ending that benign.

Those who truly understood the precarious condition of the local economy saw right away that the loss of this one man would have a dramatic impact on their town as a viable municipality. He was just that important to the community. As the owner of a good deal of leasable farmland, a string of rental houses and farms, a blacksmith's shop, a slaughterhouse (the one located behind his grocery store), a feed business, the J. D. Harmony Dry Goods and Grocery Store, and several other commercial operations, he and his wife Della had been among the town's most prosperous and reputable citizens.

Harmony's unseen but nevertheless essential and pivotal role in the local economy was that over the years he had become a financier—a de facto banker, if you will—behind the core of businesses, farms, and various entrepreneurial activities that were the backbone of Hoffman.   His activities were critical in terms of keeping their town up and running, especially now that the economic decline had gotten bad enough for banks all over to have already failed.   Too many farm towns like theirs had already dried up and blown away.   The average citizen had no way of knowing about all of this, but about everybody sensed how important Harmony had been to the well-being of the community.   People slowly began to realize how correct others were in saying that he would be impossible to replace.   While some understood this better than others, all of them were united in mourning the good man's passing.

— 25 —

THE DISGRACE OF
COLONEL CAINE

RESPECTED MERCHANT J. D. Harmony's untimely death due to the pointless shooting that happened inside of his own store led to Colonel George Jackson Caine's ruin as a businessman in the town of Hoffman. It didn't happen overnight, but it happened, just the same. More than anyone else, he had goaded Tom Shipley and Preacher Parker to fight, and it was he who had gone for the gun in Tom Shipley's hand, intent upon using it to murder Neal Easley. Everyone knew he could no more be held legally accountable for what happened than anyone else, but they also knew that his obnoxious and intemperate behavior had been the root cause of the whole event.

The Colonel denied having had any such intention, claiming that all he wanted was to keep Shipley from using the weapon to shoot Preacher Parker or for anyone else to get hurt. Not a single person who was there that day believed him. It was apparent to every one of them that if those two things had not happened—goading Tom Shipley and going for the gun— the shooting wouldn't have happened, either. Every witness had seen the look in the Colonel's eyes, and nobody had any doubt about what he would have done if the scuffle had gone his way.

The firsthand witnesses were convinced that they knew exactly what had caused the incident, so they went out of their way to make sure everyone in town knew it as well. Not too long thereafter, indignant residents popped up all over town, each one of them angry about what had happened. As would be expected, the direct focus of their anger was none other than Colonel George Jackson Caine.

As far as the more civic-minded residents of Hoffman were concerned, the Colonel had finally gone too far. His role in instigating the shooting was a transgression they could not and would not forgive, and it was their lack of forgiveness that hastened his final business failure in their town.

Feelings on behalf of Mr. and Mrs. Harmony were so strong that the Colonel became a pariah overnight. People were so upset over the loss of their favorite son that they behaved toward him as if he had gotten away with cold-blooded murder. Very few of them had ever had any respect for him, anyway, but to a person they had admired and looked up to J. D. Harmony. Their take on what had occurred was as uncomplicated and as straightforward as that.

Although it wasn't overtly or expressly articulated, the prevailing sentiment was that George Caine was one ruffian who damned well deserved to be taught a lesson. Residents acted on their beliefs, too, in a way that he found excruciatingly painful. Without saying a word to him about the shooting, through social cold-shouldering and, of course, refusing to patronize any of his business activities, they made their feelings known.

Because it happened when the local economy was in a steady decline, the refusal of most residents to engage in any further dealings with him was a brutal blow for the Colonel. He was already up to his neck in a struggle to stay financially afloat, which meant that their very pointed but unspoken message was the last thing he needed at that moment. When the loss of patronage began to drive his receipts even lower, it marked the beginning of the end of George Caine's once highly successful business operations in the town of Hoffman.

— 26 —

THE COLONEL
SPIRALS INTO DECLINE

THE COLONEL'S GREATEST PROBLEM was that the economic woes plaguing the entire country had gotten even worse in Oklahoma and, more specifically, in Hoffman. He had hoped to be able to hang on until the local economy rebounded and conditions got back to normal, but the prospects of that happening weren't looking good at all. The whole area was drying up around him, and he was hanging on by a thread.

Most residents of Hoffman—including, of course, the Colonel himself, who had not been paying as much attention as he should have—didn't fully realize that a great deal of effort was being put into saving their town. They were indirect—and in certain cases, direct—beneficiaries of various New Deal programs the Roosevelt administration implemented during the middle and late 1930s to combat the harrowing effects of the Great Depression and Dust Bowl.

These truly were years during which the unspoken law of the land could be accurately encapsulated by the gritty admonition to "Root, hog, or die!" and when conditions became bad enough for our president considered it necessary to deliver his famous series of "fireside chats." American citizens really did need to be advised during Roosevelt's inauguration that they "had nothing to fear but fear itself," and Hoffmanites, because their area was so hard hit, needed this advice more than most.

Under one *alphabet agency* heading or another, the Roosevelt administration created programs designed to get the federal and state and local economies back on track. These programs took on one or the other of three basic forms—relief, recovery, or reform, and the most immediate need around Hoffman was for jobs that could be filled by unskilled laborers, the class of persons who made up the largest percentage of the relief rolls in Oklahoma and its northeastern and nearby counties. Luther Caine, George's youngest son, would have been in this group during his own early years, if the Colonel hadn't chosen to help him out.

Local and regional construction projects conducted under the aegis of the WPA program did indeed help many Hoffmanites weather the worst of the economic storm, but, in the end, they weren't enough to bring their town back to life. From the '30s onward, Hoffman continued to wither and fade. Because there weren't enough farm or business or industrial employment to provide dependable local job opportunities, even those who would have preferred to stay in the area were eventually forced to think otherwise.

They had no choice but to move away in search of new ways of making a living.

It was at first school consolidation and then the actual closing of its public schools that killed off Hoffman for good. The town's fate was sealed when the high school had to be shut down at the end of the 1940-41 academic year. The grade school stayed in operation years longer, but, eventually, it, too, had to be shut down. Without convenient access to public schooling for their children, even more families moved out of town, and, when they did, new families couldn't be drawn in to replace them.

After many of the people who lived at Hoffman moved away, most of the town's businesses began to struggle for survival. The Colonel, somehow managed to hold on to enough customers to keep Caine's Barbershop and Cardroom up and running and marginally profitable, but his business, too, was in danger of going under.

Eventually, economic conditions deteriorated to the extent that local tax revenues dropped too low to cover the cost of such basic public services as police and fire protection. When that happened, citizens who remained in Hoffman voted to disincorporate their town. With this action, Hoffman ceased to exist as a functional municipality.

The Colonel was already at wit's end when the J. D. Harmony shooting of 1943 took place, but it became the straw that broke the camel's back. It had already become clear that, try as he might, he wouldn't be able to hang on much longer anyway. Everything he'd worked for 30 years to accumulate was about to be lost. He thanked his lucky stars for every customer he had at the time, especially for those who were so addicted to his offerings that they were willing to let their families live in shacks and allow their kids to go hungry rather than give them up. Without men of their kind, he knew for a fact, he wouldn't have been able to draw in enough income to butter his bread.

The imminent possibility of losing his means of earning a living wasn't the only problem the Colonel had to confront in the wake of the shooting. Ghosts in his closet had to be dealt with as well, in that the downside of having neglected his wife before she passed away and his children thereafter had really begun to haunt him. He was alone and without family backup during a time when he was in desperate need of exactly that kind of support, which left him with no choice but to face up to having been an abysmal failure at a man's most important roles in life—being a good husband and a responsible father.

His kids, he realized, would never be of any help to him, since he had never really been there for them. Even Luther, his youngest son, whom he had been closer to than any of the others, couldn't be of help to him in the way a favorite son might have been under normal circumstances, since they no longer had a relationship at all. The Colonel had no idea what was going on in Luther's life, and Luther had no idea what was going on in his. He didn't even know that Luther had gotten married, much less where he was or how he was doing.

During this interval of need, he began to realize the errors of his past ways. When it rains, as they say, it pours, and that's what was happening to the Colonel: A whole lot of rain had begun falling in his already deeply troubled mind.

Back when Harmony's Barbershop in Hoffman was renamed Caine's Barbershop and Poolroom in 1914 and renamed again as Caine's Barbershop and Cardroom in 1916, George Caine knew he had found his calling in life, his means of becoming a wealthy man. He was only a leaseholder and operating manager at the time, but he took for granted that the business would be his one day; and, as the future played out, that's what eventually happened. From that point forward, his time and attention had been focused on making sure the business succeeded and prospered.

He married his Creek Indian wife Bonnie Marie Tiger—or Tiger, as she was called—in 1913, and they had their first child two years later. They had five more children over the years, the last one being Luther. Things had fallen apart at home because he was preoccupied by work and because he had had absolutely no interest whatever in child rearing. He had played no role when it came to naming their children, and he had paid even less attention to caring for them after Tiger died. Because he considered raising kids to be a woman's work, he had delegated all responsibility for it to Tiger.

Tiger had had no choice but to do as she was told, but he saw now that she certainly hadn't done it enthusiastically or well. Because she resented being treated as a workhorse rather than as a member of a team of mutually responsible parents, she had made little effort to put her shoulders to the wheel. Oh, she weaned and raised the children through their early years, but she didn't do any more than she had to after that. Instead, she pushed her older kids to take on as much of responsibility for them as they could, well before they were even close to being old enough to do so. The older kids did help the younger ones, at least to some extent; mostly, though, they allowed them to run wild, just as their mother had before them. The Colonel ignored every one of them to focus on growing his business.

As the kids were coming up, the older ones did indeed provide essential support for those who were younger, but only because they felt they had no choice. Because they were rough kids and all but one of them were boys, they, like their mother, resented being pushed to perform the greater part of a role they should have had to take on alone. They didn't know the first thing about nurturing other kids, for the obvious reason that they had never experienced it themselves.   Conditions had gotten even worse for the kids after Tiger died, due to George's having continued to ignore them.

It finally dawned on the Colonel that ignoring his marital and parental duties had been short-sighted and foolish, and now, there he was, having to count the costs.   It was nobody's fault but his own.   In creating all kinds of problems for his wife and children, he had also created an enormous amount of misery for himself. Now that the chickens had come home to roost, all he could think about was the error of his ways, and this was the kind of thinking that eventually turned him into an exceedingly miserable man.

George Jackson Caine ended up responding to his disgrace in the town of Hoffman by holing up in his home, unhappily licking his wounds and trying to figure out what he ought to do next.   He had never been one to take defeat lying down, but even he could see that it would be impossible to bully his way out of his current predicament.   Whenever he stuck his head out in Hoffman, he was cold-shouldered by most everyone—including many of his former cronies, who had quickly noted that, for the Colonel, things had changed in a big way.   It couldn't have been any clearer to them that most Hoffmanites didn't want to have another thing to do with their former boss.

His business, which had been already about to collapse due to the local economy being in the doldrums, began doing even worse after the Harmony shooting. His income dropped like a rock. Nursing a whole raft of murderous thoughts, he responded by silently cursing everyone who cursed him. Sadly for him, he found that he had quit a lot of cursing to do, now that it had become apparent that no one was about to forgive him for having egged on the argument that led to the death of Hoffman's most civic-minded and beloved citizen. It had become crystal clear that people were never going to forget what happened.

Because Harmony genuinely was a man who couldn't be replaced, citizens took it upon themselves to make sure George Caine knew it. As one wag put it to emphasize the differences between them, "Fifty Colonels throw'd in a tow sack wouldn't equal the weight of one J. D. Harmony!" This comment, concisely, epitomized how most townspeople now looked at him. Their attitude had an immediate and substantive effect on his ability to do business in Hoffman, as well as a highly negative impact on the market value of his various properties.

Things had been going poorly for the Colonel before the shooting, but afterwards they became too depressing to contemplate. His means of earning a livelihood was on the verge of going away, right before his eyes. Just thinking about it sickened him to the extent that he was hardly able to get a wink of sleep at night. It wasn't just *what was happening* that was shocking; it was also *how fast it was happening.*

It had become clear that for his business and various side activities, the prosperity of the past had was about to end. Beside himself with anxiety, he tried to sell off property as a means of staving off furthers losses. That didn't go very well, and it didn't go well for one very straightforward reason: There were too few takers. Conditions were deteriorating for everyone, but they were going badly even faster for him due to his soiled reputation. Once again, he had no choice but to sell off his real property assets for much less than what they had been worth only a few years before, just as he had had to do back when he sold his farm.

He struggled along for another year or so, draining his savings and doing everything he could think of to stay financially afloat, but it was all to no avail. Declining income eventually forced him to give up on all his business pursuits in Hoffman. It was a bitter pill to swallow, but there wasn't much of anything he could do about it. It was the end of the many years of financial success he had experienced as a self-employed businessman. On the upside, though, at least as far as the Colonel was concerned, Neal Easley's business went bankrupt too, just a few years later.

Once his business went under and he didn't have much to do, the Colonel retreated even further into the confines of his home. In equal measures angry and distraught, he spent much of every day trying to drink away the burden of his regrets. Hard drink didn't help, of course; all it did was make things worse. From that point forward, the Colonel had no choice but to continue living off savings he had stashed away when he was doing well. Although he had enough saved to get by on, social ostracism and his hermit-like existence turned him into a shell of his cocky former self.

When he finally got sick and tired of seeing hard looks on the faces of people in Hoffman, he sold his once very desirable home for a pittance and moved eight miles away to nearby Henryetta, where he bought another nice home, one that had a white picket fence around it and flags growing on both sides of the concrete walkway that led from a low front gate up to his new front door. Once again, things looked good for him on the outside, when he really wasn't happy at all on the inside.

After his business went bankrupt, George Caine gradually slid downhill personally as well. Lapsing into depression and alcoholism, he existed for the remainder of his life as a recluse. Upon turning into a total alcoholic, he lived more like a hermit in a cave than as the prosperous retiree he would have been if he'd had a decent reputation. The possession of a sizeable bank account did indeed enable him to enjoy a life without need during his old age, but only for a while. No matter how much he had stashed away, it wasn't enough to keep him from becoming a bitter old man.

Much to his disappointment, his savings didn't last for as long as he had hoped they would. Unexpected health problems and uninsured medical expenses ate up so many of his ill-gotten dollars that he went broke before he died. During his final years, he ended up becoming what he'd spent his whole life desperately trying to avoid; a penniless man.

— 27 —

THE DEATH AND LEGACY OF COLONEL GEORGE JACKSON CAINE

GEORGE CAINE SETTLED in the Hoffman area just prior to the years of rapid growth that occurred after land in the Oklahoma Indian Territory opened for outside development. Following an unsuccessful attempt at farming, he moved into Hoffman proper in search of a new opportunity. That opportunity materialized when he became involved in the operation of a barbershop, a business he gradually took over and then expanded into additional areas through the use of unethical strong-armed tactics that became a modus operandi for all of his future endeavors.

He rode the crest of an economic boom that continued throughout the 1920s, capitalizing on the advent of the townsite development period in Oklahoma. After achieving a level of financial success that exceeded his own initial hopes and expectations, he was brought low through his own hubris. Then, when he was already having problems keeping his business afloat, the role he played in the shooting death of revered local leader J. D. Harmony accelerated his financial downfall. In all probability, he would have gone under anyway, due to the economic decline that began in the 1930s and continued through the 1940s, but the incident hastened and ensured his demise and turned it into a humiliating defeat.

Upon his death on March 3, 1955, at the age of 73, he was buried at the Hoffman Cemetery, in a plot next to his wife Tiger's. He had prearranged his burial, and there was no service. Not a one of his children or former fair-weather friends even knew he had died. Even if he had wanted his kids to be notified, it couldn't have been done: He hadn't kept up with any of them, which meant he had no records to show where they lived.

By the date of his mortal departure, the town of Hoffman was no more than a memory of what it once had been. After being all but destroyed by the ravages of the Dust Bowl and Great Depression, the advent of mechanized agriculture and the consequent movement of working people from farm to factory finally finished it off. After that, a combination of fires, tornados, and the vandalization and salvaging that inevitably occurs when buildings are left unattended ravaged what was left of the place, until not a single commercial building and just a few abandoned homes were left standing in his former hometown. Following all this, the town, like the once dreaded Colonel himself, was no more. Today, those who might want to have a look at Hoffman would be disappointed, since there's nothing left of the old town to be seen.

So, it was in this bitter way that Colonel George Jackson Caine's earthly journey ended. He died without any money in the bank or having any property in his name, but he left behind a very real legacy, anyway. His legacy was his six children, whose experiences in life, due as much as anything to his own inexcusable neglect of them while they were young, had long-lasting and devastatingly negative effects on future generations of his own lineage. As a means of pointedly illustrating how his behavior had an awful impact on his children and grandchildren, the life experience of just one of them, his youngest son Luther, is outlined in the pages that follow.

— 28 —

A YOUNG MAN
MARKED FOR LIFE

LUTHER JACKSON CAINE and his brothers and sister were raised in Hoffman, which was a town so small that everybody knew most of what there was to know about everybody else. Not only did people know one another, they knew one another's fathers and mothers, brothers and sisters, aunts and uncles, cousins, and in-laws as well, in some cases for as far back as three generations. On top of that, they knew one another's preferences, foibles, and shortcomings, along with every sin or transgression any one of them had ever committed. Colonel Caine and Tiger's six children grew up in just this kind of fishbowl.

From the beginning, there were multiple strikes against the Caine kids as residents of Hoffman. The first strike against them was that they were raised, as has been described, in a home that was devoid of the love, nurturing, and guidance children need during their formative years. Growing up, they had none of that, and it showed. The second strike against them was that they grew to young adulthood as the children of a locally notorious bottom feeder, a man who was gossiped about as a matter of course. That the kids were hurt by this was more a matter of guilt by association than anything else, but it caused others to think less of them, just the same. These two notable problems combined to make life much more difficult for the children than it ordinarily would have been.

Because their father was locally disreputable, many of their neighbors (although they would never have admitted to doing so) assumed that his kids would turn out to be the same, and that his youngest son, Luther, due to personal problems and inclinations that had been obvious from an early age, was likely to become the worst of the lot. It was clearly unfair to stereotype the kids in this way, but it happened just the same. All too often, kids became what their neighbors thought they would become in Hoffman, and that's all there was to it.

Once a young person got *labeled* their label placed them in a box, and, once they were placed in their box, it was next to impossible for them to get out of it. Any mistakes they ever made were never forgotten, and their mistakes were trotted out as needed to keep them in their proper place. This was a problem for all the Caine kids, but it was truer for Luther than for any of his siblings, since it was common knowledge that he had openly admired his scandalous father and wanted to be just like him, while the other kids had not. With this image of him lodged in their minds, people took for granted that Luther would grow up to be the spitting image of his infamous father, Colonel George Jackson Caine.

It was a bad break for the kids that they had received only a minimal level of parenting and nurturing from their mother Tiger, but conditions got even worse for them after she died unexpectedly on July 1, 1931, when she was only 48 years old. At the time, her children were aged 16, 14, 13, 11, 10, and 8, with Luther being the youngest. Upon her passing, sole responsibility for raising them to adulthood had fallen to their father, who had no interest, skill, or experience in child rearing at all.

When it came to being a good role model for his kids, George Caine, as might be surmised from the lifestyle he led and his means of making a living, had fallen far short of the mark during the years that followed. In fact, he was the opposite of a decent model for his kids, in that he was about as indifferent to their welfare as any parent could have been. He was a caregiver in name only, a father who done only what he absolutely had to when it came to raising the children he and Tiger brought into the world.

He provided a house for his kids to sleep in and made sure they had clothing to wear and food to eat, but that was the whole extent of his involvement in their upbringing. Beyond the basics, he provided them with no parental attention to speak of. His children raised themselves. A minimal amount of unsure care was grudgingly provided for the younger kids by their older brothers, but they had been no more committed to the task than their parents.

The kids got by on their own, with each one of them coming and going as they pleased. Although they became a wild and unruly bunch, somehow or another each of them finally made it through childhood and reached their late teenaged years. Luther was the most undisciplined of the lot, mainly because his younger years were lived out in the center of the milieu that has been described. In the words of one person who was aware of what was going on within their home, "Their daddy used a leather belt to whip the hide off them kids on a regular basis, but it never did no good, especially when it came to that youngest boy, Luther. From a young age, he was always a real problem."

Among the many adverse consequences of having been raised in a disordered home was that none of the kids received anything close to the level of emotional support or guidance they needed. The most conspicuous result of this was that the kids never bonded or grew close to one another in the way that siblings normally do. Instead, they fought and argued like wildcats, until one by one each of them learned to get by through their own devices and to live separate lives. They had no other choice, so they did what they had to do, just to get by.

As soon as George Caine's oldest son Walter thought he could make it on his own, he left his family home in search of a better life. He didn't tell anyone where he was going, nor did he say what he intended to do when he got there. He just left, without saying a single word. Doing anything, anywhere, he had decided, would be better than living one day longer than necessary in his soulless family setting. The boy really wasn't even close to being mature enough to head out into the world, but that's what the unhappy young man did.

Once the older boy set the pattern, the next four of Luther's siblings in line did the same thing: In turn by age and without leaving behind a word of explanation, they departed their family home in search of something better, thinking, as Walter had before them, that anything they might encounter would be better than the sterile life they lived at home.

Departing without notice and without explaining where they were going was the only way the kids had to take a slap at their father as they walked out the door, their only way of letting him know how they felt. He'd never paid any attention to them while they were at home, so they figured he wasn't owed any special consideration from them as they left.

The Colonel had had no objections to or qualms about his kids taking off on their own, since he thought it was just as well and he knew he really wouldn't miss them, but it aggravated him all to hell that they snubbed him as they left. Because he had fed and clothed them and kept a roof over their heads until they were old enough to depart, he thought he deserved at least some gratitude and credit for his effort.   When he didn't get it, he reacted by labeling his kids unappreciative wretches.   He damned well hated being snubbed, no matter who did it, whether it was done by his kids or anybody else.

The only one of George and Tiger's half-dozen children who wanted to make a go of it in Hoffman was Luther, and his only reason for wanting to stay in town was that he was more troubled and confused than the others.   Although he went to great lengths to make others think otherwise, he had absolutely no idea what he wanted to do with himself in adulthood, which, to his way of thinking, was approaching all too rapidly.

When it came to constructive thinking, Luther's mind, regrettably for him as well as for those with whom he came into contact later in life, was as blank as a slate.   He had more personal problems than could be enumerated, problems that caused him to make a whole string of bad choices.   His choices had an enormously negative impact on his own life and even worse effects on those who became his significant others in maturity.   In fact, his choices had such devastating effects that from this point forward, attention must be shifted to the various events and escapades that made up this young man's tortured life.

*****

Every one of the six Caine kids endured a miserable childhood and youth, again due to circumstances over which they had absolutely no control. Each one of them had problems, but Luther had the hardest go of all. His unusual traits, quirks, and odd beliefs practically guaranteed that that would be the case. One thing that could be taken for granted about him was that he would manage to find a way to cause trouble, in one way or another, for anyone he was around.

Those who knew him well had predicted all along that he would have to contend with all kinds of issues as he moved from youth to adulthood, and they couldn't have been more correct. From the day he was born on March 29, 1923, he had enough problems to assure an extraordinarily trying childhood for himself as well as to have plenty left over for his late teenaged and young adult years. He most definitely was not an average young person.

Luther's many personal problems stemmed from his having been totally incorrigible as a child, a kid who was difficult to deal with from an early age. Comments provided for this story confirm that he grew up behaving in accordance with the town folks' unspoken script, in that he seemed determined to carry on in just the way locals thought he would. Because he was the Colonel's son, they had always assumed he would behave much like his father, and that was exactly what he did, to the extent that every step he took seemed calculated to make his neighbors seem more prescient than they really were. "As the twig is bent, so grows the leaf," folks said of him, as they shook their heads in resignation.

When he began to feel poorly treated at school, for example, after a while he just stopped attending. He preferred to hang around with other young miscreants, boys whose attitudes were just like his own, and this behavior, as would be expected, resulted in his growing up uneducated and unskilled. As a result of running around with ne'er-do-wells who routinely devoted most of their waking hours to experimentation with smoking, gambling, drink-ing, carousing, and other forms of socially undesirable behavior, it wasn't long before he fell prey to every single one of these vices, as if it were a matter of course. This mode and pattern of behavior only worsened as he grew into his late teenage and early adult years.

One of Luther's most unusual hang-ups was that he hated his own mixed racial heritage. Although he was half Creek, he looked fully white, and, because he wanted to see himself as white, he tried to make sure everyone he knew thought he was white as well.

Not surprisingly, the way in which he processed all of this led to subliminal confliction over his own racial identity, and this, when combined with how strongly he identified with the tough-guy image his father always maintained, had the effect of making him even more bigoted than he already was. His problem with his Indian mother was that she had never been a dutiful parent, and he held that against her, blaming it on her heritage.   His white father, the Colonel, had been far more neglectful than she was, but for some reason this highly pertinent fact never entered his mind or had any impact at all on his way of thinking.

Like his brothers and sister, Luther raised himself within the confines of the local white society. Eventually, he adopted the attitudes and values of his white buddies, which amounted to yet another step backwards, due to their being so bigoted that they couldn't see straight.   Before he finally quit school, he had convinced himself that having Indian blood was the major cause of his own poor personal discipline, lax work ethic, destructive habits, and generally poor grasp on life.   He was so prejudiced that he failed to develop the sense of self-respect that ought to have been his as a birthright.   Because he had no respect for Indians or blacks, he seemed to dislike a part of himself, which, of course, made no sense at all.

It isn't surprising that Luther ended up as bigoted as he was, given that he grew to adulthood in a town and at a time when racial separation was the norm and overt segregation was firmly entrenched. Although the population of Hoffman was about equally divided between whites, blacks, and Indians, blacks and to a lesser degree Indians were never accepted as the equals of whites in local society. Extreme racial prejudice was something young people of all races came by honestly in their area, very early on in life. During Luther's formative years, it was like this in most rural farm towns in the South—and, for that matter, in most of the country.

Segregation wasn't directly spoken of in Luther's day, but the terms of racial interaction were understood by everyone in town. Whites and blacks and Indians readily mixed for commercial purposes—they all traded at the same stores, sold their cotton at the same gin, and so on—but unspoken expectations and norms prevented the races, especially blacks and whites, from mixing on equal terms in schools, churches, restaurants, barbershops, and other ordinary settings.

Whites lived on the north side of town, while blacks, who were very straightforwardly called coloreds or niggers, lived on the south side, in an area most every white person, from old grannies to truculent teenagers, routinely referred to as Niggertown. Blacks of the era, it must be pointed out, used equally offensive, thoughtless, and insulting words to refer to members of the white community. The bigotry and ignorance that existed in their setting, and it was there in abundance, was widely distributed among the races.

The local Creek Indians used graphic terms of their own to refer to their white and black neighbors, but they could and did mix much more openly with blacks than most whites ever did. In Luther's day, there were plenty of instances of intermarriage between Indians and blacks and whites and Indians, but marriage between blacks and whites rarely ever happened. The latter was not just frowned upon; it was codified as an illegal act.

From the standpoint of most whites of his area, anyone with any discernible black heritage at all was completely and forever black. The interbreeding of people of different racial types was no more of an accepted practice in Hoffman than it was in most other parts of the country. Plenty of local whites even frowned on intermarriage with Indians, but it often happened, nevertheless, and many happy marriages came of it. From that point forward, there have been Oklahomans who are proud to point out their American Indian heritage.

Having grown up in such an environment, Luther ended up becoming a profoundly prejudiced and bigoted man. Long before he was mature enough to give the matter any rational thought, these harmful values were ingrained in his psychological makeup. Racial prejudice was so deeply embedded in his psyche that he didn't even know it existed. He never gave the matter any conscious thought; it was just a given. This way of thinking became yet another significant nail in his own coffin, in that it caused all kinds of problems for him in later life.

Nothing about Luther's childhood, adolescent, or young adult years was pleasant or picturesque; instead, these stages were abysmal messes for him, from the first days of them until the last. His rise to adulthood seemed choreographed to demonstrate that great truth resides in the old maxim that the sins of the father are visited upon the son. Luther got off to a rocky start, and, after that, things never stopped heading in a downward direction.

The bitterness within him gradually morphed into an unusual form of involuntary resentment, a negative attitude of mind that handicapped him even more than he already was. Those who tried to describe his behavior during his late teenage and early adult years said that he was not *deranged* as much as he was *unarranged.* "That boy," one of them said, "should never be described as deranged, because that would imply that he once had a normal set of attitudes and values, when he never did; his values were never in good order in the first place."

Luther's acquaintances and relatives knew that most of his issues sprang from the way he was raised—or, more accurately, from *the way he raised himself.* Because he'd had no genuine parenting to speak of, it was reasonable of them to assume that he would have to contend with all kinds of issues as he rose to adulthood, and even more thereafter. Their assessment was right on the money; as an adult, he had more problems than he knew how to shake a stick at, and then some.

No one ever understood Luther's underlying mental and emotional condition, least of all Luther himself. Some even conjectured that he may have suffered from some sort of unknown and therefore never accurately diagnosed problem or illness that damaged him before he left his mother's womb—fetal alcohol poisoning being one such theory. Both of his parents had been drinkers, and things like that do happen, more often than commonly realized. Again, though, after the fact, there's no sure way to tell.

The only thing that was known for sure about Luther is that whatever level of nurturing he received as he was coming up, there hadn't been enough of it to be effective. From the day they are born, some kids just don't have a chance, and Luther seemed to be one of them. In all fairness, anyone, not just Luther, would have had a tough time trying to live a responsible and orderly life after being raised in a home as arbitrary and chaotic as his.

The deficiencies of Luther's upbringing eventually proved to be too great of a challenge for him to overcome, as evidenced by the fact of his collapsing under the weight of them later in life. Who knows, though; he may have been one of those human beings who wouldn't have been able to adjust to society under any set of circumstances, even if his childhood and youth hadn't been as unguided as they were. There are people like that, from all sorts of backgrounds.

In the end, though, all that mattered was that when he reached young adulthood, he was beset by a whole raft of personal problems he didn't understand and had no idea how to deal with. To the extent of near paranoia, he never trusted anyone. He thought everybody was out to take advantage of him. This way of thinking added a whole new level of difficulty to his life, and it led to perpetual problems in terms of how he dealt with authority, even that which was legitimately exercised. In the same way that he had had difficulty getting along with teachers and administrators during the few years he was in school, he found it tough to cooperate with supervisors and coworkers later in life. This problem increased in severity with every experience he had in the workplace, until it became extremely hard for him to hang on to any job.

Being encumbered by a host of deep-seated emotional hang-ups made it impossible for him to create and maintain a healthy personal life, and he was too paranoid and suspicious to allow anyone to help him work out problems before they got out of hand. These difficulties practically destroyed his chances of becoming a self-sufficient, productive adult.

It quickly became obvious to most anyone he was around that Luther was becoming more reckless with every day that passed, even to the extent of his not giving any serious thought to what might happen to him later down the line. He lived for the moment, even as he brooded over his need for a better way of life. All he ever seemed to notice was that others were enjoying lifestyles of the kind he wanted to live, while he wasn't. His overall dilemma was that he just couldn't figure out how to go about building better conditions for himself. Because he was always on the lookout for quick fixes and easy ways out, he never figured out that good things must be worked for and earned in an ethical way.

Following his father's example, he turned at an early age to hard drink as a means of anesthetizing himself to the difficulties of everyday life. There was nothing to prevent a young man of his time from hanging out in any bar he wanted to patronize, not if he had ready money and wanted to be there badly enough. His having taken to the party life with ease and abandon hadn't surprised or upset his father in the least, since he had done—and, at the time, was still doing—the same thing himself. Because he'd been just like his son when he was a younger man, he figured the kid would surely grow out of his problems of the moment and eventually get things under control.

Even as a teenager, Luther had already begun to go through life looking for escape and relief whenever and wherever he could find it. He had a well-established habit of hanging out in bars, plus a well-deserved reputation for coming home drunk on a regular basis. Partying and boozing and carousing until the cows came home had become his favorite refuge, and his course in life was irretrievably set.

— 29 —

LUTHER AND HIS DEPRESSION

WHEN LUTHER CAINE turned 13 in 1936 and began living out his party-hardy teenaged years, our country was in the middle of the Great Depression and the Dust Bowl. Because his father, the Colonel, was keeping him financially afloat, he was able to carry on in ways that most young men of his area couldn't begin to afford. He went where he wanted and did as he wanted, always trying to ignore the over-all economic condition of his area and behave as if conditions were better than they really were. It didn't work. The impact of the great economic events that were taking place had been impossible to ignore, even for a slacker like him.

Economic problems were widespread in and around Hoffman, and Luther saw enough of them to intensify his already serious insecurities. For the majority of those who lived in his part of Oklahoma, the 1930s through '40s were unusually stressful years. There's no doubt that for the rest of his life he remembered what he saw, just as there's no doubt that it had to have had a significant impact on his way of thinking.

Luther grew up a witness to poverty conditions extreme enough to have had adverse effects on the way he thought about a whole range of things.   Due to his father's assistance, he got along okay personally, but he observed personal, family, business, and institutional failures as they occurred and saw instances of poverty, inequity, indebtedness, and hopelessness all around him.   He most certainly would have noted that only a lucky few of his neighbors had the wherewithal to live without want, while the majority had barely enough to get by on.   He was insulated from personal privation, but it had to have been a depressingly smothering atmosphere in which to come of age, and he had to have felt just a little bit guilty.

The Depression was the longest and deepest economic downturn in the history of the United States. It lasted more than a decade, beginning in 1929 and ending during World War II in 1941.   The Dust Bowl years—the years of extended drought, unusually high temperatures, poor agricultural results, and wind erosion that impacted our country's midwestern states— overlapped the Depression years, adding an additional layer of economic misery.   Before the Dust Bowl was over, hundreds of thousands of farmers, especially from Oklahoma, Arkansas, and Texas, were forced to move elsewhere, most often to California.

These simultaneous events had devastating effects on Oklahoma and, more specifically, on the part of the state where Hoffman was located.   Plenty of gloomily depressing old newspaper articles and photographs exist to document how difficult these years were at Hoffman. Judging from looks on faces and the way they had to dress and what they had to do to survive, many of them became more ragged and hardened during this bleak and trying experience. It couldn't be any clearer that those who lived in or around the town of Hoffman, including Luther Caine and his father George, were totally unprepared for a crisis of the magnitude of the one that hit them.

In its location eight miles east of the town of Henryetta and about 70 miles south of Tulsa out near a depot on the KO&G Railroad line, Hoffman had gotten off to a quick and promising start after it was incorporated back in the early 1900s. Early arrivals had been enthusiastic about their prospects, and Hoffman was routinely described as "a nice town in which to live." During the oil and coal boom of the early and mid-20s, the number of people living in or around the general area ballooned to over 2,000, which was quite a respectable figure for the early days of rural Oklahoma. Looks on the faces of people photographed during this period confirm the feelings of optimism and confidence that prevailed before the so-called "Dirty Thirties" rolled around.

Those who were drawn out to the Indian Territory had to have been at least to some degree risk takers, since many of them gave up the certainties and comforts of living in more settled cities in search of an opportunity to own their own land or build wealth in some other way. The early settlers of Hoffman came in with high hopes of cashing in on the excellent opportunities that were promised by promoters, developers, and investors. Colonel Caine, for example, moved there for that very reason. In his day, most people considered Hoffman to be an up-and-coming town, one with great prospects for solid future growth.

Unfortunately for many if not most of those who settled in the Hoffman area intent on making the town or its environs their permanent home, things did not pan out the way they hoped. Even before the emergence of the Great Depression and Dust Bowl, a good number of the early arrivals who generated a lot of the early positive buzz about the area had proven to be temporary rather than permanent residents, people whose intent all along had been to make a quick buck. *Land churning*, as it was called, was a big business in and around new towns like Hoffman. These people extracted as much profit as they could, and then moved in search of new opportunities. Secondly, many of those who landed in or around the new town due to the oil and coal boom of the early and mid-20s eventually moved away as well, when job opportunities in those fields nosedived in later years.

The departure of these folks marked the beginning of a chain reaction decline that accelerated in speed and intensity with the onslaught of the Great Depression, the Dust Bowl, and reversals in the local farm economy. As economic conditions continued to worsen during the 1930s and '40s, more and more businesses, farms, and ranches around Hoffman failed.

From its incorporation in 1905 until around 1929, economic conditions around Luther's hometown were as good as they ever got. By the time he reached his teens in the mid-30s, many of the farm farms in his part of Oklahoma as well as many of the independent businesses that had been the backbone of Hoffman's once promising downtown had either already failed or were locked in the same struggle to hang on that had beset so much of the rest of the country. It can be documented that economic conditions around Hoffman got even worse than they were at most other locations. In the same way that it snuck up on folks all around the country, the economic decline that occurred during these difficult years caught Luther and George Caine napping.

As the 1930s and '40s ground slowly by, more and more local businesses failed, typically through an agonizing process of slow financial strangulation. Among the entities that went under (some after closing once and then reopening under different names) were the Hoffman Herald Newspaper, Myer's Bank, the Farmers' and Merchants' Bank, the Ideal Hat Shop, the Square Deal Grist Mill, Kinyon's Dray and Transfer Line, Brown's Lumber Company, Jones's Feed Lot, Rush's Lumberyard, Farrell's Grocery Store,

Herman's Grocery, Stevenson's Grocery, Hoover's Grocery Store, Dr. Hudson's Office, Dr. Carloss's Office, Stackhouse's Drugstore, Carloss's Drugstore, Dick Lewis's Law Office, Buchannan's Hardware, Embalming, and Picture Show, both hotels (the one with a ballroom and the one without), Frank Wilson's Livery Stable, Jones's Feed Store, Simpson's Blacksmith and Garage, the Schultz, Carpenter and Varner Mercantile Store, Ritterhoff and Gates Mercantile Store, and a range of other businesses, ranches, and farming operations. In later years, both schools that served the town (the one for whites and the one for blacks) and Hoffman's rural post office were shut down as well.

Cotton had been about the only cash crop raised around Hoffman since its earliest days, with local farmers doing business with the Choctaw Gin Company or the Berge and Forbes Company. Both gins were opened shortly after the town was incorporated, and they had been in operation ever since. Farmers were able to earn some returns from this cash crop, but most of them, after the farm economy tanked, didn't fare well enough to hang on. Eventually, both gins started having trouble making ends meet, and they, too, went out of business.

Farming and ranching had been by far the most common means of making a living among those who settled around Hoffman, just as they were in most every area of the country when Luther was coming up.

Even in the best of years, the dry land farming practiced in his isolated area had always required a back-bending amount of hard work and a whole lot of cautious optimism. Now, though, conditions had become impossible, at least for many of those who made a living in these ways.

It had to have come as a crushing blow to every rural farmer who finally realized that, even after all his diligent effort, his farm, like those of so many of his neighbors, was also going to fail. It isn't difficult to imagine the sense of desperation that must have overwhelmed these hardworking folks, who knew there was nothing else around that they could turn to as a means of making a living. Only a few of the luckier farmers and ranchers were able to sustain commercially viable operations; the majority struggled just to eke out a basic existence, and many, as it turned out, weren't even able to do that.

Large numbers of the early settlers of Hoffman had gotten their start, in whole or in part, as tenant farmers or sharecroppers, hoping, of course, to move on from there to owning and operating plots of their own. What ended up happening, though, was that most of them stayed too poor to save enough capital to buy land, which meant that they ended up stuck as perpetual tenants or sharecroppers, whether they liked it or not. The economic decline made their prospects even more hopeless than it already was.

Under the system that had prevailed from the beginning at the town site, many farm families worked under contract with a landlord. They were temporary land users who agreed to pay for the use of the land with a share of whatever crops they produced. Landlords often helped their tenants get started by supplying them with land, a mule or mules, and a shack to live in, but, beyond that, they were usually left to their own devices. Since most of these folks had little to no money, they had to buy their groceries, seed, implements, and other necessities on credit at stores that were as often as not owned, at least in part, by the same landlords who owned their farms. Some local merchants even coined their own money in those days, cheap metal coins that could be exchanged only at their stores.

Arrangements of this kind, of course, had always been far more rewarding for merchants and large landowners than for those who operated on a smaller scale. It was a system that effectively locked many families in a cycle of debt and struggle that they could never work their way out of, one in which the crops they produced each year were often mortgaged far in advance. Year after year, many of them found that the value of their produce was less than the bill, plus interest, that they ran up at their local store. It was much like an old-fashioned indentured or master-slave relationship, one that poor people didn't understand and from which they were effectively powerless to escape.

Tenant farmers who operated on leased or rented land were often not much better off than the sharecroppers, even before the hard times of the '30s and '40s. Many of them stayed just as deeply in debt to local landowners and merchants as the sharecroppers, barely making a living. The prevailing laws and customs were such that tenant and sharecropper families were effectively prevented from leaving their rented homesteads if they owed money to anyone. Many were never able to dig their way out of debts that tended to increase with each passing year, and they became trapped in the system. For some, this cycle was broken only after they were effectively forced off the land by the collapse of not only farm prices but the entire system of family farms that occurred during the depression years. Hoffman was just one of many farm towns throughout the country that suffered through a catastrophic economic decline during this long string of ruinous years.

Growing up in Hoffman, Luther saw failure and destitution all around him. His whole section of Oklahoma was undergoing a major economic reversal. Even during good years, making a living as a dry land farmer in his area would never have been described as easy, but now prospects for farmers had become even more desperate. People who'd barely been making ends meet now had to deal with the phenomenon of the underpinnings seeming to have dropped out of the whole national economy. It had to have been enough to drive a poor man into abject despondency.

These awful economic conditions emerged before sufficient and effective social safety net programs existed to help people ride out the economic mess they were caught up in, and that's why so many people became so desperate so fast. The domino effect chain of economic failures that was happening all around the country was readily observable at Hoffman, and what residents of the area were seeing must have made them feel that their situation was utterly hopeless.

The effect of all these events on farmers and farm laborers and, in turn, local merchants and other professionals who were indirectly dependent on their income was devastating. Even as the Great Depression and the Dust Bowl were in full swing, the economic viability of family farms in towns like Hoffman was being further undermined by the industrialization transforming the country, specifically in the form of large-scale mechanized farming.

The combination of the problems caused by drought, economic depression, reduced need for agricultural labor, and the competitive inefficiency of family farms brought on by agricultural mechanization effectively forced large numbers of people to leave Dust Bowl states like Oklahoma to search for work elsewhere. It was during these years that the majority of those who were trying to escape from what was happening in the Midwest came to be referred as *Okies*, despite many of them being from states other than Oklahoma. Because the largest proportion of them really were Oklahomans, the term was a reasonable fit. As he progressed through his teenage years, Luther had no way of knowing that he would soon be caught up in this very phenomenon.

Even though he had been sheltered from the worst effects of the economic recession by his father' support, Luther still couldn't escape being enormously troubled by Hoffman's decline. These years had to have been extremely depressing, if only at a subconscious level, given that he and his father were living in the middle of one of the hardest hit areas of their state. His father's business, Caines's Barbershop and Cardroom, was barely hanging on, even with the Colonel doing everything he could think of to keep it up and running and at least marginally profitable. By this time, his father had eliminated every one of his side means of making money. His main lines of business—the barbershop, bar, grill, gambling, betting, and lending—went on as before, but on a notably reduced scale.

Even as he was struggling to stay afloat, the Colonel had continued to subsidize Luther's bacchanalian lifestyle, maybe because he felt guilty about having ignored his other five kids. Luther, as would be imagined, had been more than happy to remain a beneficiary of the Colonel's largess for as long as he could. He had no idea how dire conditions had become at his father's business. In blissful ignorance, he continued to live the same fancy-free lifestyle he had in the past.   For as long as he enjoyed his father's support and lived at home, this was how life went on for him.   Outwardly, it seemed that had everything under control, but, inwardly, he was just as troubled as ever.   His overarching problem was the same as always: He still had no idea what he wanted to make of himself.   For those who live in an unreal world, figuring that out can be a major problem.

— 30 —

LUTHER CAINE, A MAN ABOUT TOWN

LUTHER CAINE GREW UP to become a young man who loved to drink and smoke and party into the night, every night. He continued to do all he could to portray himself as being footloose and fancy free, a person without a care in the world, and there's no doubt that he conceived of himself as exactly that. Those who truly understood what was going on with him, however, looked at his situation in an entirely different light. He wasn't fooling anybody, they said, because they knew he hadn't a clue in the world what kind of man he wanted to be in adulthood, much less how he was going to earn a living.

Few of those who contributed information for this account of his life knew much of anything at all about how things went for him after he got married, but they sure didn't mince words when it came to describing how he carried on while he lived at Hoffman. Due to his many personal problems, they said he did some truly crazy things. He wasn't just youthfully blithe or occasionally irresponsible, they said; he was off-the-wall irrational. As one of those who remembered him put it, "That boy never had all of his oars in the water, that's for damned sure."

Luther's aimlessness may may have stemmed from nothing more than the relief he felt after finally getting out on his own and away from a cold and unsupportive home environment. He very well might have felt that way, just as his siblings had before him. Being singled out as his father's favorite ought to have made him a happy young man, but, for some unknown reason, it didn't. Even though he had been favored with enough wherewithal to enjoy many long and carefree evenings of aimless fun, it was never enough.

One of his closer acquaintances put forth the most concise and accurate description of his mental state anyone offered when he said, "The boy just thought he was a no-count person, somebody who'd never amount to nothing, no matter what he done. He must have decided that, if that was the way it was gonna be, then, hell, why not just go ahead and make the best of it and have fun while you can. He didn't see no further than the immediate here and now, and that's all there was to it. For him, there wasn't no tomorrow that needed to be worried about!"

At the risk of putting words in his mouth, it seems clear that what this acquaintance meant was that Luther had talked himself into believing that he had no hope of ever achieving success in life. Because he had never found peace in the past, he doubted that he ever would in the future. He believed there was no good reason for him to be optimistic about anything. Because he was convinced that he wasn't as good as everyone else, his manner of thinking became fatalistic. He believed he was destined to crash and burn, no matter how he might try to avoid it. The distorted logic that guided his conduct seemed to have been "When you know you're going to fail anyway, why bother striving for anything better than what you have at the moment?"

End results are never automatic or inevitable in life, but Luther behaved as if he thought they were, as if he thought he was doomed from the outset. Some kids have lived through childhood agonies as bad or far worse than he experienced and survived them unmarked, while others have suffered lasting emotional damaged after far less traumatic experiences. Luther, it seems clear in retrospect, was one who had been traumatized by his childhood experience. His damage wasn't outwardly observable, but it was still debilitatingly real.

He never stopped trying to fool others into thinking he was doing well, but it is clear in retrospect that he never quite managed to con-vince himself. Because he was never able to find his own private peace, a perpetual state of discontent became part of his mental makeup. Down deep inside, he was an inexplicably maladjusted and unhappy person, and he thought nothing could be done to change his fundamental self or his basic circumstances.

When he lost the will to act positively on his own behalf, his life took a serious turn in the wrong direction.

Fatalism, a low self-image, and unspecified anxiety seemed to have prevented him from trying to improve his own condition. Having no self-esteem is usually accompanied by having no personal discipline either. Being beset by these conditions led to self-destructive behavior on his part, behavior that others—neighbors, acquaintances, employers, teachers, would-be friends, and others—found inexplicably frustrating.

The will to act positively and proactively on his own behalf seemed to be absent in Luther. Because he thought he deserved the angst and misery of his day-to-day life, he was an exceedingly unhappy young man.

Try as he might to hide his many problems, Luther's efforts were in vain: Most people saw right through him, no matter what he said or how he tried to conceal his problems. It was next to impossible to portray himself as a carefree person in Hoffman, anyway, since the town was so economically bad off that it was about to dry up and blow away. It's hard to convincingly portray oneself as a man about town when there's almost nothing left of your town to go about.

It was as a means of running away from his personal problems that Luther began ranging from town to town in pursuit of something he never was unable to define. He caroused the beer bars and honky-tonks of Muskogee, Checotah, Okmulgee, and other nearby cities on a regular basis, until a bar and dance hall called Tuley's about 50 miles away over in McAlester ended up becoming his favorite haunt, mainly because it tended to be livelier than most of the other places he frequented.

The women Luther met at the time were just as much into drinking and partying as he was, but the majority of them could see that he was about a mile wide but only an inch deep in terms of actual substance. But, because he had at least some spending money on hand (due to the Colonel's largess) when many other young single men of that time did not, they partied with him willingly, even though they knew better than to take him seriously. Even so, he was a good-looking, devil-may-care, insouciant young man, which meant that he would eventually meet a woman of genuine interest to him, and it was at Tuley's Pavilion in McAlester that it finally happened.

Luther was not a man most eligible young women would fall for and want to take home to meet mom and dad, and he most definitely wasn't a young man Mr. and Mrs. Dexter Hicks of McAlester, Oklahoma, wanted their attractive and talented daughter Pirley Mae to take up with. As they say, though, opposites tend to attract, and that was undoubtably what happened shortly after Pirley Mae Hicks got acquainted with Luther Jackson Caine.

— 31 —

A YOUNG WOMAN
WITH PROSPECTS

THE HICKS WERE a hardworking, extremely conservative, highly religious couple, and they had worked hard for the good things they had in life. They had a charming home in McAlester, the county seat of Pittsburg County, where they were passionately committed to and deeply involved in the affairs of their Christian fundamentalist church. The values their church espoused were near and dear to their hearts, and they most definitely were not Sunday Christians.

More than anything else, the Hicks were extremely proud of the accomplishments of their beautiful, talented, and religiously committed daughter, Pirley. Since childhood, Pirley had been an enthusiastic participant in the affairs of their congregation, where she had been involved in singing and choir practice from an early age. She enjoyed singing more than any other activity, and she was clearly good at it. Her parents had always been especially pleased by her abilities and accomplishments in that area.

Pirley was a tall, thin, outgoing, attractive girl, a vivacious young woman whose greatest fortune in life was to have been born into the arms of warm and caring parents. She was popular and appealing enough to have had her choice of any one of a series of suitors from among the young men of her congregation and the larger community, but her heart was set on pursuing a career in music before settling down.

From an early age, she had been told that she had an excellent singing voice. She and her parents considered it a blessing that distinguished her from others. They were pleased that it had been good enough for her to become a member of a gospel music quartet at church as well as gain a spot with a local quartet, one that was active within the community at large. Because they were available for hire to sing at weddings or anniversaries or other special occasions, the second group became well known in their region. In addition to performing at various events, they also sang once per week during the gospel music segment of a half-hour live hometown country music program broadcasted by a local radio station.

Pirley was irrevocably committed to becoming a professional entertainer, and she was convinced that she was good enough to earn a living through her vocal abilities. More than anything else in life, she wanted to build on her past and current accomplishments and move onward and upward toward better venues within her chosen field

Having any amount of radio experience made her something of a standout within her congregation and hometown, since recognition of that kind didn't happen very often. Her limited but nevertheless inspiring contact with the music business left her star struck to the extent of becoming convinced that she was good enough to earn real recognition as well as some hard money through her musical talent. According to her relatives, she had become obsessed with this ambition. They thought the dream was strong enough to have become the most significant driving force of her life.

They were right, too: The goal of becoming a recognized country music singer really had captured Pirley's imagination, to the extent of her having committed to it, lock, stock, and barrel. She was so obsessed by her dream that she was unable to think of anything else.

According to her relatives, Pirley Mae eventually became bored to tears by the highly conventional and religious home life her parents expected her to live. She craved an opportunity to break free from a routine she had come to think of as stifling and intolerably dull. What she wanted, in a word, was *excitement*, and, because time was so rapidly slipping away, she became ever more willing to take a few chances to make sure she got it.

Pirley's basic problem was that there were too few opportunities for a reputable single girl to be different in a remote town like hers. That's surely why she got to feeling as bottled up as she did. Acceptable behavior for women—especially for those who were young and unmarried—was a lot more circumscribed at that time than it is today, and this was especially so for females in her social circle. It isn't hard to imagine how she must have felt, especially if she really did have a marketable degree of talent as a singer.

Her relatives all agreed that her downfall began shortly after she made a first trip to Tuley's Pavilion, a country music dance hall and bar located out on the throughway near the outskirts of town. Even today, most parents in her area wouldn't welcome an attractive young daughter becoming associated with any outfit of its kind, but this feeling had to have been doubly true back when the dancehall was going strong. Her religious and highly conservative parents absolutely hated the place.

Tuley's had a reputation for being one of the most wide-open and uninhibited dancehalls around. One of Pirley's uncles said it was so unruly that even those who went there to drink and dance on occasional weekends didn't hesitate to run it down. "It wasn't nothing but a shabby honky-tonk," he said, "but there wasn't no other place in town to kick up your heels, so we went out there from time to time anyway. We shouldn't of, but we did!"

Most young single women in Pirley's circle of friends wouldn't have dreamt of patronizing Tuley's, and few upright ladies of any social circle would have considered going there alone. To them, that would have been akin to wearing a sign on their backs, advertising easy availability. Members of her family, looking down and away and dejectedly shaking their heads as they spoke, said that Pirley Mae had chosen of her own free will to do both, and that, as far as they were concerned, was behavior beyond the pale. Pirley's parents and members of their church felt the same way.

Pirley gravitated toward Tuley's because it was the only venue in or around McAlester that had any interest in hiring what was referred to in the trade as a *girl singer*. One was needed for the country music band they sponsored for live entertainment at the dance hall. Immediately after hearing about the opening, she took off after it in hot pursuit.

Ignoring her parents' unequivocal opposition and pointed warnings, she made up her mind that she was going to audition for the job, and, once she made her commitment, that's all there was to it. There was nothing they could say or do, she told her parents, to dissuade her from trying out for the opportunity.

"You ought to stay away from that dump," her parents argued as forcefully as they could, "or you'll wind up in more trouble than you ever dreamed possible!"   Wringing their hands in desperation, they pleaded with the daughter they loved so dearly to reconsider.

Pirley, though, turned a deaf ear to everything they said. In truth, she didn't *want* to believe them, despite having a sinking feeling down deep inside that what they were saying was most likely true. Her problem was that she was far too caught up in her dreams to admit it.

Various family members readily recalled the friction that sprang up between daughter and parents during this trying interlude.   In the end, though, Pirley chose to ignore her parents' advice and pursue her own interests. Obviously, attempting to reason with a strong-willed single young woman was no easier back then than it is today.

Pirley was dead set on pursuing the only opportunity she knew of to hone her talents as a singer enough to move onward and upward to better options, even if it did happen to be offered by one of the more unsavory establishments in their part of the county.   Like a moth attracted to a flame, she felt compelled to show up for a tryout, no matter what her parents advised.   From her perspective, Tuley's was nothing more than a stopping-off place, a convenient setting for her to get started in the music business.   From there, she hoped to move on to bigger and more lucrative—and, hopefully, more respectable—venues at some point in the future.

When she tried out and landed the job, Pirley was thrilled beyond measure. She thought it would be her launching point, but it really wasn't as much of an accomplishment to be hired by Tuley's as she imagined, since the addition of almost any fresh and beautiful young female face to the group that performed out there would have been a welcome sight.

Tuley's had anything but the kind of happy environment that drew in crowds of fun-loving and cheerful patrons who enjoyed good country music that Pirley Mae wanted to think of it as having. Her becoming involved in what went on out there was more akin to casting a pearl before swine than she could envision.

Her parents, as would be imagined, were absolutely appalled by the commitment she'd made. They didn't consider singing at a dump like Tuley's a step up for their talented daughter; to them, it was a giant step backwards.

Her first few weekends of singing before a crowd as a member of a true country music band turned out to be every bit as much of a thrill for Pirley as she thought it would be, but then, unexpectedly, just as her enthusiasm peaked and she was ready to spread her wings, the whole gambit at Tuley's had suddenly fallen apart. After only a short string of performances, the band folded up after several of the lead musicians decided that the gig didn't pay enough to be worth their time and effort.

When the lead musicians threw in the towel to take on regular jobs, other members of the group bailed as well. With that, Pirley's dream was crushed, leaving her feeling sick at heart, even to the extent of near despondency. From her perspective, it felt as if the whole band had effectively walked off and left her there, sitting high and dry, entirely on her own. She had a burning desire to boogie, but they didn't.

In a heartbeat, involvement with Tuley's had turned into a classic instance of her being all dressed up, but with no place to go. For her, the band's breakup was a huge disappointment. She had hoped with all her heart to make the best of the only opportunity she had ever had to hone her talent as a singer with an active group.

It was a discouraging setback, but Pirley was far too fixated to give up on her dream of pursuing a career in music. She remained as determined as ever to land an opportunity to become a professional singer. Her moment in the limelight had been short, but it had been an honest-to-goodness thrill. Craving more of the same, the last thing she wanted was to abandon her dream and return to her former humdrum existence.

While it was true that she had landed the only job of its kind available in the entire area, her association with Tuley's eventually turned out to be one of those instances in life when she would have been much better off if she had taken her parents' advice. They couldn't have been any more correct when it came to their assessment of the dancehall; it was a bad match for their daughter, in every imaginable way, shape, and form.

To the dismay of her family and friends, what happened after the band folded was that Pirley ended up becoming a regular patron at Tuley's. Her parents couldn't believe what she started doing, and her family members and others were more appalled by her behavior than ever before. None of them knew what to make of it.

In the words of one of her cousins, "The more that girl hung out at that grubby joint the more she done a complete turnaround. It wasn't long before she didn't want nothin' to do with her family or church anymore. She turned into a different brand of person than she used to be, and she never was the same after that. Neither her parents nor nobody else could figure out what got into her. Once she tasted what she considered to be the high life, she never wanted to let it go." Her cousin's comments weren't polished or eloquent, but his observation couldn't have been any more correct.

Pirley's mental image of Tuley's, for one thing, was quite different from the way members of her family and former circle of friends thought of the place. The term honky-tonk had a completely different meaning to them than it had to her. To her, it conjured up images of colorful musicians and singers pumping out happy music in touristy cities like New Orleans or Memphis or St. Louis, always in pleasant taverns that offered music that was earthy and real and in tune with the times.   In her locality, however, and more specifically within her former reference group, the term had no such cachet.

Within her former social circle, the term was used to refer to a different sort of establishment—a low-class, smoky beer hall, an outfit they would have associated with boozing, dirty dancing, and illegal gambling rather than a place that offered what any of them would have described as decent or wholesome entertainment.   To them, honky-tonks were cheap and sleazy dives, places often featuring back-room hangouts that were used for one illicit purpose or another.   "Pirley Mae," as several family members put it, "sure as hell went off the deep end when she got involved with Tuley's.   Her parents nearly went crazy worrying about her."

From a longer-termed perspective, her decision to get involved with Tuley's was indeed one of those occasions when Pirley would have been wise to have listened to parents.   For her, things went downhill from that point forward.   Her life would have gone much better if she had stayed on the straight and narrow path her parents started her on as a child.

— 32 —

A MEETING OF EQUALS

TULEY'S WAS JUST ONE of many bars Luther Caine drifted into and out of in the years before he and Pirley first met, joints he hung out at to drink and party and otherwise escape the realities he was unable to handle in broad daylight. She first went there only because the business had offered a viable career opportunity, but overnight it had become a regular retreat, an atmosphere in which to escape what she had come to think of as a dull and monotonous existence. More likely than not, each of them thought of Tuley's as a solitary option, the only entertainment venue in their area that offered a substitute for what they really wanted—the bright lights and cheerfulness of a more enlightened city.

It isn't hard to imagine the chemistry that must have come into play on the summer night at Tuley's Pavilion when Pirley Mae Hicks and Luther Jackson Caine met for the first time. Because they were in the same state of mind, they most likely hit it off from the beginning.

Luther was as trim and slim and as good looking as he was free-wheeling and fun-loving, and Pirley was most definitely in the market for an opportunity to let loose and party. That they were kindred spirits was obvious. Neither one was of any mind to resist what the other had to offer.

"Luther Caine," several of Pirley's relatives said, "just flat swept her off her feet, and from then on she wasn't nothin' but putty in his hands." On the other hand, Luther's fair-weather drinking friends said that "If he hadn't of met that floozy, he might have grown up enough to get his life in order." Both perspectives amounted to no more than classic instances of pots calling kettles black, a case of each camp blaming the other for what happened after Luther and Pirley got to know one another. By the time it finally dawned on them that they might be a bad match, it was too late for the information to matter.

Regardless of how their first meeting came to pass, all that mattered from that point forward was that they satisfied one another's needs exceptionally well. Pirley was three years older than Luther, but neither of them gave that a single thought. They got along so well that they pulled out all the stops and immediately decided to tie the marital knot. Seeing no good reason to wait, they moved ahead as soon as they could make it happen. They decided to get married only a few short months after their first meeting, but it was a decision changed their lives forever.

Pirley's parents, who were already miserably distraught over the path their beautiful and talented daughter had taken, were now at their absolute wit's end. They thought she'd gone completely off her rocker, and they didn't make any secret of their opinion of Luther. They couldn't stand him, and they didn't hesitate to tell her so. That, of course, led to even more alienation between daughter and parents, to the extent that she cut off all communication with them.

According to her relatives, "Pirley Mae's mom and dad thought that her new man wasn't nothin' but a dandy, a party guy who'd never done—and never would do—a lick of work in his life. They did what they could to persuade her to stay the hell away from him, but once that girl got somethin' in her mind there wasn't no way of gettin' it back out. That's the way she always was, from way back when she was just a tiny little thing. If she hadn't been that way," they said, "she'd have had a loving home long ago. At least three decent men have proposed to her, but damned if she didn't turn ever one of them down. Now, just look where that high-and-mighty attitude has gotten her!"

All anyone in Pirley's family ever learned about Luther was that he seemed so feckless and ditzy they could hardly tolerate the man. They didn't know a single thing about him or his family. They had had no time to discover that he had no family that they could learn anything about. It isn't difficult to imagine how Pirley's parents must have felt while her relationship with Luther was heating up; it had to have been heart-rending to watch their talented, attractive, and much-loved daughter slip away before their eyes.

Throwing caution to the wind, Luther and Pirley made their vows in a civil ceremony on January 2, 1941, shortly after a raucous New Year's Eve party and dance at Tuley's. Whether anyone was present to witness the ceremony, none of her relatives knew. None of them were there, not even her heartbroken parents, who had to have been aghast over not just *what had happened* but over *how fast it had taken place.* In no more than a matter of months, their wonderful life with a precious daughter had been turned upside down, and it would never be the same again.

It isn't surprising that members of the Hicks family didn't get to know Luther before he and Pirley made their commitment to one another, since they barely had time to get acquainted themselves. How could they, when their decision to marry was made less than a few months after their first chance meeting at Tuley's? If they had allowed anything close to a reasonable amount of time to get to know each other before taking the plunge, they might have changed their minds. It might have become apparent that they had far too many personal problems and were way too immature to make a serious decision about anything. There was a lot more heat between them than substance, that's for sure.

Luther had once looked up to and openly admired his father, but he departed with hurt feelings and didn't say a word to him when he left home in 1941 to marry Pirley Mae Hicks. He acknowledged and rightly appreciated that his dad had given him a starter car, helped set him up with occasional part time work, and provided him with spending money when he had done none of those good things for any of his siblings, but he was angry with him, anyway. After going out of his way to make him feel special, the Colonel had spent no time to speak of with him after that.

Even after all the Colonel had done for him—and, for that matter, what he was still doing—they had hardly ever spoken. Much to Luther's dismay, an occasional smile and a few pats on the back were all he ever got, and the reason for it was quite simple: His father was always too busy. It took him a while, but he was eventually forced to acknowledge that what his siblings had said about their father was true: His first and only genuine love was his business. Despite having been his favorite son, Luther, like his brothers and sister before him, had finally learned that there was no room in his father's life for any of his kids, including himself.

Those who provided information for this account of Pirley and Luther's life together unanimously agreed that their first meeting could not have occurred at a worse juncture for either of them. It happened just as he had become the proverbial accident ready to happen, almost as if he were just waiting for a good opportunity to become a catastrophe in someone's life, and, in turn, her family and circle of friends realized that she had become just as dangerous in her own way, in that she had become a young woman who looked at the world through rose-colored glasses.

Theirs was an ill-fated union if there ever was one, from the very beginning of it until the end. Some human combinations are so ill considered and negative that no mutual support can be derived from them, and their relationship seemed to have been one of them. It seemed obvious to others that each partner would quickly use up the shallow reserves of kindness, consideration, and love the other had to offer, leaving behind only the barrenness of their individual lives on which to build a decent marriage. Because they both were desperately in need of precisely the sort of caring support the other was totally incapable of giving, most of the people they knew would have placed the odds of their staying together as no better than one in a million.

— 33 —

MARITAL BLISS?

WHEN LUTHER AND PIRLEY (Hicks) Caine left their family homes to begin wedded life together, they rented a well-worn house located out on the main highway that went through McAlester. It was less than ten miles away from where her parents lived and where she had been raised. For Luther, their move was his last residential contact with the town of Hoffman.

They selected their new location because it was not too far from Tuley's, which was just how they wanted to be positioned. They were truly fond of McAlester, solely due to all the happy evenings they had enjoyed at Tuley's during the few months before they were married. They were looking forward to partaking in a whole lot more of the same in years to come.

Pirley found a waitressing job at a truck stop out on Highway 69, not too far from their new home and, of course, not too far from Tuley's, either. Luther, too, located an entry level job nearby, in his case at a local lumberyard, which, like where she worked, was also close to their favorite hangout. The dance hall was their unmistakable center of gravity, there's no doubt about that. Neither of their jobs paid well, but the state of the local economy was so bad that they considered themselves lucky to be gainfully employed. Job opportunities were scarce in their area, and wages were poor all over.

Luther was satisfied with the admittedly run-down old house he had been able to rent as their first home, and not just because it was close to Tuley's. He liked it because the monthly payment was low and because it was adjacent to the rental home of a former neighbor from back home, a man who also had moved from Hoffman to McAlester. Upon asking the man's name back when he was a child, the response he received was "You just call me Uncle Clarence, and that will be fine." Luther and his siblings had called the man that ever since, even after learning that the use of the term had been a local honorific custom and that Clarence was not a true birth uncle. In any case, Luther had always liked the man, who really wasn't old at all; He just seemed that way to Luther and his siblings, who were young kids. He and Clarence really weren't close, but, because they lived next to each other, they did talk, at least on occasion.

As soon as the newlyweds got settled in their rental home and income began flowing in from their jobs, they jumped headlong back into living the high life with their fair-weather friends and luxuriating in each other's arms. Being married, they thought to themselves, was a wonderful way to live.

Together, they were bringing in more income monthly than they ever had in their lives, but it didn't take long for them to realize they didn't have as much as they thought. Like many young couples starting out, they didn't have a realistic understanding of all the costs and various expenses required to maintain a household. Having to pay their own bills was a new experience for them, and it turned out to be a whole lot more difficult than they expected. They fell short very quickly, mostly because they drank, partied, and otherwise frittered away far too much of what they brought in each month.

Their combined earnings, which initially had seemed like quite a lot, had given them a false sense of security: They weren't bringing in much more than what was needed to keep food on their table and a roof over their heads. Oblivious to their true financial condition, they continued their revelries at Tuley's as in the past, believing that they had nothing to worry about. The world, they genuinely believed, was their oyster, and they truly believed they were destined to live happily ever after.

It wasn't long, as most of those who knew about their situation would have imagined, before reality began to intrude, and a whole lot of rain began to fall on their parade. And not just financial rain either; other problems cropped up as well, and, when things began to go badly for the couple, they did so in a hurry.

Pirley had known from their earliest days together that Luther was a heavy drinker and party-hardy kind of guy. It was this behavior that had drawn her to him at the outset. She liked that lifestyle, too, just as much as he did. Up till this point, though, she had never had to contend with the way Luther tended to behave when parties were over. On mornings after big bashes, a side of him came out she hadn't ever seen.

Typical weekend evenings for them began with their getting a buzz on and starting to feel happy, which was just what she liked for them to do. Luther, though, because he was a much heavier drinker, all too often kept at it until he was falling-down drunk or until their money was gone, whichever came first. At that point, the downside of that kind of behavior became apparent very quickly.

Late in the night, after they got back home, he tended to become surly if she raised an objection or tried to make a point about anything that had happened during a given evening, no matter how inconsequential it might be. Too many nights ended with Pirley learning more about Luther's nasty temperament. He started slapping her around not long after they got together, behaving as if he had every right to do so. His father had done the same to his mother back when he was a kid, so he saw nothing wrong in behaving that way himself. On top of that, he damned well didn't like her questioning him about what he did or did not do. He intended to do what he wanted, when he wanted, no matter what she had to say about it. Luther had no idea that their behavior amounted to a classic instance of family history repeating itself, but it did.

Their relationship, to say the least, wasn't working out the way Pirley had hoped, but, as strange as it may seem, she was much more accepting of the way Luther treated her than most people would think. She behaved as if she, too, believed he was entitled to treat her as badly as he did, maybe because she felt guilty about having taken up with the guy after being warned against it by every person she knew, beginning with her own loving parents. She'd complain and bawl and wail whenever he roughed her up, but she never seriously considered taking any action to make it stop. Instead, she just put up with it as best she could. It was too bad that she didn't raise a ruckus over how he treated her, since her acquiescence only encouraged more of the same.

Luther's pattern of behavior became set in stone during those early days of their marriage. He worked only as much as he had to, and then partied whenever he could, forgetting any thoughts he may have had of trying to get ahead in life or maintain a decent home.

Before long, he started stopping off for drinks at the end of every workday. After throwing back a few to loosen up, he'd drive over to pick up Pirley her when her shift ended at the restaurant. Once together, they would head to Tuley's for more of the carefree highlife that meant so much to them. This pattern, as uncomplicated as it was, ended up becoming a way of life for them, and Tuley's became their home away from home. She liked the whoop and holler night life as much as he did, so she was beside him whenever she could be. It was a way of life that pleased them both.

After a while, though, Luther began to drink so much after work that he'd either forget or just not want to bother with going to the restaurant to pick up her up. Because she had no car, this left her sitting there, fuming over having been left behind. After waiting for who knows how long, she'd ask a co-worker or a friend to drop her off at home. When Luther finally showed up, it would either be either too late or he would be too drunk for them to go back out again. Pirley didn't like being left out of anything, so she did everything she could think of to make sure Luther knew it. Whenever she tore into him, another screaming argument would break out between them, and once again they'd begin to fight like cats and dogs.

In their neighbor "Uncle" Clarence's words, "Them kids would scream and cuss and slam things around like they were ready to kill one another. It got to be the damnedest thing you ever heard. I tried my best to talk sense into that boy, but it never did no good. Talking to him until you was blue in the face never made no difference. I ended up wishing that he and that nutty wife of his hadn't moved anywhere close to where I lived. Ever one of our neighbors felt the same damned way!"

Clarence went on to explain that the couple's loud and bitter arguments often culminated in physical abuse. Neighbors knew that Luther slapped Pirley around on a regular basis, occasionally leaving her with ailments such as ringing in the ears, black eyes, a bloody nose, or bruises on various parts of her body, and it wasn't long until word of how he was behaving got back to members of her family.

It grated against her relatives to hear what was happening to Pirley in Luther's household, but, after thinking things over for a while, they decided against attempting to interfere. They knew all too well how outspoken, smart-mouthed, wild, and irresponsible Pirley had become, and they wanted to think she was being subjected to treatment richly deserved. Her husband may be in the process of doing what had to be done, just to straighten her out. Several members of her family were known to have said that they would have loved to have kicked her butt, too, if they could have done it without getting thrown in jail, solely because of the misery she had caused her dutiful parents.

A few members of her family and the couple's immediate neighbors—Clarence, for example—knew what was going on in the Caine household, but in their part of the country it wasn't considered appropriate or, for that matter, healthy, to interfere in what went on within another family's private home. It was up to Pirley and Luther, they believed, to work things out in their own way and on their own schedule. Because they were just a young couple, others assumed they would get things straight after a while.

No one truly appreciated how severe Luther's abuse of Pirley became as their time together flew by. They didn't just have fights in the way people normally conceive of domestic arguments, as differences of opinion between members of a struggling relationship. "No," said Clarence, "that's not the way it was between them fools. The truth," he said, "was that Luther slapped the living hell out of her, not just ever now and again but on a regular basis."

Predictably, things started to fall apart for the couple only a few years after they started living together. When Luther's hangovers got so bad that he started missing work, he was fired from his job at the lumberyard. Shortly after that, Pirley had to tell Luther she was pregnant with their first child. Not too long thereafter, an increasing number of their bills had to be left unpaid, and creditors began to hound them day and night.

Then, when Pirley had to quit her job at the restaurant due to feminine problems that arose prior to her delivery date, they found themselves in overwhelmingly dire financial straits. It happened, to their way of thinking, before they knew what hit them, when it had been coming at them like a freight train for as long as they'd been married. They had gotten into a financial hole so deep that there was no conceivable way of digging themselves out of it. Wringing their hands in despair, they had no idea what they were going to do.

Then, after allowing the couple to get several months behind on paying their rent, the man they were renting from finally decided he, too, had enough, whereupon he started hounding them to pay up, just like everyone else they owed money to. Their grocery store and utility bills were overdue as well. Later, when Pirley's time came, they incurred yet another large debt, in this instance for medical services and a short stay at the public hospital following the delivery their first baby.

"There's no doubt about it," said Clarence, "they were in a pitiful mess, especially after they brought home that poor baby. They seemed like kids having kids, when they didn't even have a pot to pee in themselves. I wanted to help them out, but, hell, I didn't have nothin' extra myself. Things was so damned bad back then, nobody had much of anything, much less anything extra. I was still drinking a lot at the time, before I finally settled down.

Then," he said, "one day as I drove by their house, I saw the front door standing open and the shades of the windows slung back. It looked like they'd been evicted, but I found out later that that wasn't what had happened. Hell, no," he said. "They'd loaded up and skipped out, just to get out of paying their bills. The guy who owned the property told me all about it. Nobody knew where they went; they just packed up what they could get in their car and took off, without leaving behind a word about where they were goin.' Let me tell you, there were plenty days when I was so flat busted that I wanted to do the same damned thing myself. People don't understand how hard it was to get by at the time. There wasn't any work to be found!"

— 34 —

LUTHER AND
PIRLEY DISAPPEAR

VERY FEW OF HER limited family contacts or acquaintances heard much of anything from Luther or Pirley from that point forward, and the only news they did receive came in bits and snatches. On occasion, they would pop up unexpectedly by means of a phone call or a letter with no return address, but then they would disappear all over again, just as quickly as they showed up. Even if someone had wanted to contact them, there would have been no way to do so.

It seemed obvious to those they touched bases with on occasion that the couple had no intention of reestablishing any ongoing interaction, clearly because they didn't want to expose themselves to the possibility of being tracked down. They knew very well that if they could be located, it would more likely than not result in their being hauled off to jail for skipping out on their debts.

Luther and Pirley tried to be subtle about what they were doing, but it was abundantly clear to everyone that they were trying to evade the law. Because her relatives didn't want to get involved in anything of that kind, this became yet another rationale for them to avoid any further contact with either of them. On his side of the family, there were no relatives who gave a hoot what they did, one way or the other. His father George Caine over in Hoffman didn't even know his son had gotten married.

A few years thereafter, the couple went further underground than ever before, even to the extent of their rarely ever being heard from again. They stopped sending messages altogether, but by then it no longer mattered, since members of her family had long since given up on them as a lost cause. There was no evidence that showed any of her relatives lost any sleep over Pirley's absence, probably because by that time she and Luther were fully estranged from all of them.

To describe Luther and Pirley's situation in the bluntest of terms, they weren't missed by anyone, and some of her own relatives weren't shy about declaring that their departure for parts unknown was no big loss to any of them. From their perspective, it was just as well that they were gone, since they'd never been anything but trouble, anyway. It was unlikely that any of her relatives would have done anything to help them, even if they had asked, since they had burned their bridges long ago. So, that's how things were left to stand: Not a single member of her family knew—or, for that matter, cared to know—what happened to Luther and Pirley after they ran off.

— 35 —

LIVING ON THE EDGE
OF DISASTER

JUST AS MEMBERS of her family suspected, Luther and Pirley Caine resolved their financial problems in McAlester by skipping out of town late one night in a great hurry, leaving behind not only a landlord who had been dunning them for months of past due rent but also a whole list of other angry creditors. It was their first use of this approach to dealing with financial exigency, but over the years that followed they honed their use of it to perfection. There wasn't anything fancy about what they were doing, but it worked, and it worked time and time again, at one location after another.

After leaving McAlester, they first landed about 85 miles away in the city of Tahlequah, arriving with a new mouth to feed, no home to stay in, and not a single dollar of income coming in. They were in a serious fix, of course, one bad enough to have been upsetting to anyone. Because they were living out of their car, they had to have been worried sick.

Luther, though, because he was a resourceful schemer, got his family out of immediate trouble by working out a rental deal on yet another old house, in this instance one in such bad condition that a desperate landlord allowed them to move in on terms of *rent due in a month.* With rental terms like those, it's not difficult to imagine what the house had to have been like: It had to have been a complete dump.

After dealing with their housing problem, Luther's next challenge was to find a new job. He knew he had to get after it, since he and Pirley were only steps above being flat broke. While he went out in search of work, she stayed home to take care of their new baby, Johnny Ray Caine, the son who was born to them just prior to their hasty departure from McAlester. His middle name was the same as his paternal grandfather's.

What was most significant about their move was that it forced Luther to face up to the truth of just how woefully unprepared he was to be a bread-winner even for himself, much less for his two needy dependents. Now that the Colonel was no longer around to subsidize his profligate lifestyle, he had to get serious about finding a niche in the world of work. The rubber, as they say, was about to meet the road. He had no idea how to go about making a living, just as past acquaintances and neighbors had noted when he was single. It was at this point that the long list of personal problems he had to contend with began creating life-long difficulties for his new family.

Luther's basic hang-up was that he really wasn't all there when it came to interacting with others for any practical purpose—searching for, landing, or holding down a meaningful job, as immediate cases in point. Soon after any focused and meaningful job interview got off the ground, he had an ungovernable tendency to shoot himself in the foot. The minute his negative attitude and unusual quirks became clear, conversations tended to go downhill in a heartbeat.

Even the most reasonable of questions about his past or habits or values, questions of the kind to be expected in most any interview, could be enough to stimulate a defensive, combative reaction, often one strong enough to make any evaluator hesitant about adding him to a work team. His body language and general tactlessness were clear indications that he not only resented any questions about his personal life but also documented a highly argumentative personality. This finding led to frequent *thanks but no thanks* responses on the part of prospective employers.

Most job applicants intuitively understand that employers will be put off by any response to a standard question that is needlessly evasive or pointlessly combative, or both, but this never seemed to occur to Luther. He had such a bad attitude it was easy for most interviewers to see that, as an employee, he would stir the pot at every opportunity. His overall demeanor was more of an open confession of his many personal problems than any direct comment he might have made.

That he was poorly educated and had no specific job skills to sell was painfully obvious, and his overall visage also further dimmed his prospects. He had been tall and lanky as a teenager and young man, but he had grown up to be a husky, hulking man. Guzzling beer from day to day, as would be imagined, brought that about, just as it does for many men. He was big enough to be intimidating when there was a scowl was on his face, and there was an inappropriate scowl on his face most of the time because he clearly wasn't a well-adjusted man. It would be fair to say that he looked obnoxious, irritable, and angry because he was just that—obnoxious, irritable, and angry. It was impossible not to notice. All these attributes made it next to impossible for him to land a job in any work setting that involved groups of people.

Luther's dilemma, at least when it came to finding meaningful employment, was quite apparent: He was uneducated, untrained, argumentative, physically intimidating, and had obvious attitude problems, all wrapped up in the same package. He just wasn't the sort of man employers with other choices would want to hire. Because he was his own worst enemy, he was unemployable for anything more than entry level jobs.

Even when he was lucky enough to get hired for an entry level position where work was done in a group setting, it typically didn't take long for him to create a whole pot full of problems for his employer. Most of them found out in short order that it was a real challenge just to get him to show up on time, sober and ready to put in a full day of work. Even when he did show up in good condition, the chip he carried on his shoulder led to clashes with co-workers and supervisors alike.

If an exasperated supervisor took him to task and tried to correct his troublesome ways, the negative traits and values that were so burdensome to him would at once come into play. First, he'd act out his innate defensiveness; then he'd become argumentative; and, eventually, he'd become combative. He'd display every reaction under the sun, except the only one that was right—a willingness to accept direction, cooperate, and learn. He seldom showed anything close to the level of receptiveness to learning, amenability to correction, and cooperative behavior that a supervisor expected to see, the kind of reaction that is needed to sustain a smoothly functioning and productive workplace.

On repeated occasions, his behavior led to so much lost productivity or needless conflict, or both, that he effectively forced employers to say the dreaded words, "I'm sorry, but we're going to have to let you go." Whenever that happened, Luther would burn his bridges by cussing out whoever delivered the bad tidings and then move on in search of something else.

What all these employment-related problems meant for Luther and Pirley and their kids was that they had to live off substandard wages and endure long stretches of unemployment. Even when he did have work, he tended not to do well on the job, since he lacked any meaningful level of control over his behavior and emotions. He was, as has been pointed out, completely incapable of getting along with his co-workers and supervisors, or, for that matter, anyone else.

*****

For the next two decades, Luther bounced from one low paying job to another, never staying at any one town long enough to earn higher pay or to build up any seniority or vested advantages. Most of what he did earn, he and Pirley spent by engaging in the same level of drinking and partying they had enjoyed since they first met. It was all they knew how to do together, because it was all they had ever done. They partied whenever they could, wherever they could, and without much restraint, seldom ever paying any attention to the impact their behavior would have on their household. They had a lot of fun, no doubt, but their lifestyle kept them in dire financial straits all the time.

Whenever their financial problems got too far out of hand at one location, they'd move their family to another town and start up all over again. Dodging creditors and staying just a few steps ahead of the law became a normal and expected part of their lives. They remained "lost" from members of their extended family and others only because Luther and Pirley wanted to be lost, just so they could not be tracked down through relatives or acquaintances. Normal relationships couldn't be sustained with anyone they knew. When a family lives underground and gets by through building up debts and then running away from their responsibilities, niceties of that kind fall by the wayside.

Although Luther and Pirley's marriage was about as defective as a relationship can be and they lived in perpetual poverty, they ended up staying married, as remarkable as it may sound, for over 20 years. Yet another remarkable and near unbelievable fact about them is they did become a highly effective couple in at least one notable way—the production of children. They brought a total of 12 of them into the world, an even dozen, all born during the years they were together in their on-again and off-again union. Had her two miscarriages also carried to term, Pirley would have been the mother of 14 children.

Lousy economic conditions prevailed all over during these pre-family planning years, but that consideration wasn't enough to prevent large families from becoming as common as dirt, especially among poor people who lived in or came out of rural farm communities. The Caines, for example, were never thrilled about another child being born to them on a near-annual basis, but they accepted it as "just the way things were." What difference was there, they must have believed, between neglecting one child and neglecting a dozen of them.

Because Luther had no interest or preferences when it came to naming their children, the choice of names was Pirley's province alone. It was a task she relished, mainly because she had always hated the plainness of her own first and middle names. She hated her own family surname, Hicks, even more. For this reason, she gave each of her girls what she would have described as *French-sounding* first names that sounded as girlish and cute as possible—Collette, Claudine, and Candice. And, for reasons that only she could have explained, she gave all her boys names that ended in the letter *y*—Johnny, Arley, Freddy, Jerry, Terry, Tommy, Billy, Bobby, and Ronny. Tommy, for example, was not short for Thomas; it was an actual given name.

*****

As Luther's drinking problem worsened over the years, the couple continued to argue with a vengeance. Pirley felt shortchanged by the ever-increasing size of their family, since she was expected to stay home and take care of the pack while he (supposedly) was out trying to earn a living for all of them. She expected to be invited to any revelries he got involved in when he was at home, mainly because she bitterly resented being left alone with a bunch of snotty-nosed kids while he was out having a barrel of fun. If he left her behind, she threw an absolute hissy fit. Her constant complaining about this aggravated Luther all to hell, and it became a major cause of ongoing argumentation, second only to their financial problems.

If there was any going out to be done, Pirley's preference was for them to do it as a family. To her, doing it as a family meant taking their kids along with them when they went to a bar and leaving them to wait outside in the car while she and Luther were inside, drinking and laughing and having a great evening. It her view, it was acceptable parenting just check on the kids from time to time, occasionally delivering candy and cokes to keep them fed and happy.

What sort of trouble could their kids get into, she figured, if they were confined to their car? If they got too whiney or irritable, either she or Luther would walk out of whatever bar they were in and whip their butts, just to keep them quieted down. She knew this wasn't the ideal way to handle kids, but, from her perspective, she had no choice. It was a matter of either doing what had to be done or being left out of Luther's partying, and the very last thing

Pirley wanted was to be left out of anything. In her view, bringing the kids along when the two of them went out bar hopping amounted to more responsible parenting than leaving them at home, alone.

Pirley was as happy as a tick in later years, when some of the kids grew old enough to be left in charge of the younger ones, since that allowed her to feel much better about leaving all of them at home when she and Luther went out on the town. All the many problems that can arise when kids are left to take care of even younger kids was of no great concern to her, no more than it was to Luther.

Arguing and fighting stayed a constant in their household, even as baby after baby was added to the family over the years. In their home, such as it was, conflict was as normal and as ordinary as oatmeal, and the kids grew up right in the middle of it. Luther's drinking worsened with every year that passed, until he eventually became so besotted that alcohol permanently damaged his brain. He'd been an alcoholic for years, but at this point he went completely over the hill, and, for him, there was no going back.

The change in Luther's mental condition became a great problem for Pirley and their kids, as it turned him into an even more belligerent man than he had been all along. Now, he was deranged as well. As so often happens after an alcoholic disintegrates to this kind of low point, he began to make a regular practice of taking his frustration out on his family.

Pirley and the kids routinely wound up as targets of his increasingly violet rages. When he wasn't emotionally or physically terrorizing them, he neglected them altogether. Demanding whatever he wanted whenever he wanted it, every member of the family learned to jump at his commands; if they didn't, they knew there would be serious consequences. Luther was a father who believed in making liberal use of his belt, justifying his doing so as being necessary for keeping what he considered to be an orderly household.

Jumping around from one lousy job to another turned out to be a miserably depressing and ego-deflating way of making a living. Things were tough all over in their part of Oklahoma back when they were starting out, but they were even more difficult for unskilled and difficult-to-place men like Luther. With all his many problems, his only outlet was to take his frustration out on his wife and kids. Behavior of this kind wasn't unprecedented in their area during those difficult economic times; lots of men in his economic and social condition behaved the same way.

During the 1940s when Luther and Pirley were trying to make ends meet, prospects for making a decent living in their area had to have seemed hopelessly bleak. Very few jobs were out there to be found, and those that were available didn't pay very well. Even for semi-skilled workers, jobs had never been plentiful in their neck of the woods, but, for guys like Luther, who had no education or training or personal discipline or self-control to speak of, job prospects were few and far between. It was for this reason that it became common for men like him to hop from one farm town to another in search of work.

It would have been pointless to go back to his hometown to look for a spot, since he knew his father, the Colonel, wouldn't help him and there was no work to be found in Hoffman, anyway. Economic opportunity was so lacking there that more than a few people were going to bed hungry every night. Nor could he go back to McAlester or Tahlequah or to other towns in their region of the state, since he owed money at multiple locations and creditors would have been on him in a minute. Luther had to have been an extremely worried man, knowing that he could be tracked down and brought to justice in a heartbeat, no matter where they lived on a given date. He and Pirley existed on a financial razor's edge, always so short of money that they didn't know from one day to the next how they were going to get by.

Like many of his contemporaries, Luther combed his area of the state in search of any work that could be done by an unskilled laborer. When nothing could be found, he started doing the same thing that others like him began doing at the time— he joined the procession of people traveling out west to states like Arizona and California in search of seasonal employment.

Lots of men with backgrounds like Luther's left Oklahoma in search of work during these difficult years. They had to try something, even if it turned out to be wrong. Because they had heard rumors that jobs could be found in California, that state became a favored destination for many of his contemporaries. Even field or orchard work, most of them figured, would be better than what they could find where they were, which was next to nothing, and, even when they were able to find work, they couldn't make a good living. Most of them made exploratory trips at first, leaving their families behind as they checked on conditions out west.

*****

As years passed, Luther made the journey from Oklahoma to California again and again, always to do agricultural work in the San Joaquin Valley. He irrigated fields, thinned, swamped, or picked fruit, hoed rows, or picked cotton, and did many other similar jobs. When work ran out in one town, he moved on to the next. He worked in towns large and small throughout the Valley, towns such as Arvin, Poplar, Porterville, Fresno, Visalia, Hanford, Bakersfield, and others. It was in this way that he got to know the state.

As ragged as his life at home in Oklahoma had been, it had to have been a real challenge to spend many months at a stretch away from familiar surroundings and living in communities where people like him weren't always wanted or made to feel welcome. There is no way that being forced to become a migratory farm worker could have been an uplifting experience. Other people just like him were doing the same thing, also because they had no other choice.

Some men were so negatively affected by what they went through during these grueling years that they remembered them for the rest of their lives, and it seemed clear that for Luther working as a transient farm laborer was yet another devastating blow. In his case, it seemed to have exaggerated his already highly pessimistic mindset and brought about an even greater sense of personal disorientation and anomie. It certainly wasn't an uplifting experience,

Back at home, conditions were just as miserable for Pirley. When he was away, she had to take care of all their kids by herself, which was a maddening and thankless task. She got them by through using whatever money he left behind or mailed home, taking advantage of public handouts, and by otherwise fending for them as best she could. It was never easy.

She and the kids often had to do without, especially during the family's later years in Oklahoma, when Luther's trips out west began lasting longer and longer. When he returned home after being away, Pirley, who became more unstable during every one of his absences, was always about ready to jump out of her skin due to having wrestled every day for months with a wild and uncouth bunch of ill-behaving, yelling, hungry children.

Whenever Luther returned home, he and Pirley would revert to their former pattern of behavior as quick as a wink. Because some of the kids had grown old enough to be left in charge of the younger ones, she took advantage of it to get the two of them out the house as fast as they could make it happen. Leaving their brood in charge of the oldest and toughest child who happened to be at home, they'd head out for more nights of drinking and partying.

*****

After making the trip out west again and again on his own during the 1940s, Luther and Pirley eventually began to travel together out to California to do seasonal work in the fields. Whenever they did, they'd pull the kids out of school, load everything they could carry into whatever old car they owned, and then head out, usually with no more than a minimum amount of cash on hand to get them wherever they were going. Upon reaching their destination, they would camp under a bridge or live out of their car, always after getting as close as possible to the orchard or field in which they had found work. When the work ran out at one location, they'd move on to another; and when work ran out for the season, they'd use whatever cash they had on hand to get them back to Oklahoma for the winter.

This stayed their pattern until 1952, when the Caine's finally loaded up all their kids and whatever belongings could be carried in their car and headed out to California yet again, this time with the intent of staying there for good. Pirley had insisted on it, knowing that she couldn't stand any more of Luther's long absences.

Upon arrival in California, they landed at a collection of farm labor cabins found on the outskirts of the San Joaquin Valley town of Porterville, a privately owned business called Hood's Camp. The camp was nothing more than a cluster of 10 by 18-foot frame cabins that had been hastily thrown up as temporary housing for farm laborers, people just like Luther and Pirley. In addition to the cabins, the camp had a mini-sized grocery store, a one stall garage, a ragged-looking used car lot, and a communal restroom facility, one that featured the first shower and flush toilet to which the Caines had ever had access. The operation was owned and managed by a no-nonsense couple by the name of Hobert and Ortha Hood.

From the camp, Luther and Pirley and their children would leave each morning to do farm labor piecework such as picking or hoeing cotton, pulling bolls, cutting lemons or oranges, cleaning fields and orchards of weeds and pie melons, or whatever else needed doing.   The kids, even the babies, were taken to the fields with the rest of the family.   Every member of the family who could work did.   As soon as they were able to do anything, the kids were put to doing something.

Even so, it was a real chore for the family to make a living as farm laborers, since they were poorly paid for work that was never dependable.   It is easy to imagine that on many occasions Luther and Pirley must have longed for the good old days of their early married life back in rural Oklahoma.

*****

Another harmful consequence of Luther's pervasive drunkenness was that he routinely gambled away a good part of any income he was able to earn in the farm town beer joints he frequented, dives that were much like the one his father ran back in Hoffman.   The bars he spent time in kept up cardrooms, places where guys like him could forget about their troubles for a while and dream about winning big. They never did, of course, because the house always had the upper hand.

Losing much of his already low earnings in this way left Pirley and his kids in increasingly desperate straits at home. It was common for them to have way too little to eat, and what they did have was usually of the poorest quality and nutritional value. Their kids were often flat out hungry. This, among other things, is part of what it means to be neglected as a child.

The financial problems of Luther and Pirley's household continued to worsen as years passed, until things finally reached a breaking point, a time when abject poverty looked them in the face. It was a Godsend when bags of food and boxes of secondhand clothing occasionally appeared on their doorstep. It was manna from heaven for the kids, who, although they may have known in the backs of their minds how the items came to be there, were way too deprived to look a gift horse in the mouth. Whether goods arrived there due to pity on the part of thoughtful neighbors or the action of one local charitable agency or another didn't even cross their minds; all that mattered to them was that it was there, and that it kept them from having no clothes to wear and going hungry.

When their parents were *out*—which was as often as Luther and Pirley could scrape together enough money to get through the door—the kids were left at home to fend for themselves. Luther went by himself when he could, but Pirley never let him leave her behind if she could help it. Wherever the action was, that's where she wanted to be. It didn't bother

her any more than it did him that they left a pack of young and hungry kids at home; both were equally neglectful.

While their parents were away, the younger kids were cared for—to the extent that they were cared for at all—by the older ones, who were, of course, left to write their own rules and standards of behavior. At their age, the older kids were anything but enlightened in terms of parenting skills or meeting the fundamental needs of their younger siblings. The smaller kids grew up being subjected to child rearing techniques that have been practiced since the beginning of time—threats of mayhem, whacks on any conveniently accessible part of the anatomy, and swift kicks in the butt, which is the level of "care" that too often occurs when kids are left in charge of raising other kids and which was only one of many bad things that could have happened to them. It would be right to see that Luther Caine's household exemplified how negative family dynamics often carry over from one generation to another.

It hardly needs to be said that the kids grew up in an emotionally barren home, one in which family-based activities, social involvements, or spending on frivolous items like newspapers, magazines, or books was never even considered. They were children for whom personal care and attention had never existed. All the traditional holidays and special occasions that are celebrated in the households of families that have young children were totally ignored in theirs. Birthdays, for example, went by without a whisper.

*****

As conditions in the Caine household deteriorated, the nights when Luther came home stumbling drunk became fearful occasions for Pirley and the kids, whether she had been out with him or not. Returning to their ragged place and having to face a gaggle of cranky, needy, hungry, squalling brats brought out the worst in him, probably because it was at these moments when he was most pointedly reminded just how bad he had allowed their home life to become.

Luther tried to find more and better work, but for people like him not too many avenues for making a decent living were out there. His ill-kept appearance, glaringly negative attitude, and the ever-present cigarette that dangled from his mouth served only to limit his options, due to his manifesting all the attributes and habits necessary to make him a virtual poster boy for the commonly held stereotype of a shiftless, lowlife Okie. In later life, he became a passable self-taught auto mechanic, mainly because, in that profession, he could work on his own and stay away from other people. Having built up this skill made him employable by various independent garages, but only when he could manage to stay sober enough to work for a reasonable length of time at a given location.

Luther eventually deteriorated to a point where he lost all control over his drunken tirades. He continued to vent his rage on any member of the household he could reach, which made him more dangerous than ever. There were occasions when over the most minor and meaningless of provocations, he'd beat Pirley in front of the kids. Using either the front or back of his hand, it wasn't uncommon for him to blacken her eyes, bloody her nose, or create large bruises or swellings. The younger kids stood by cowering and sobbing on numerous occasions as he beat their mother to the floor, sometimes hurting her so badly she couldn't get up.

If one of the older kids did or said anything to intervene, their father would turn his rage on them. He slapped or hit or kicked them around the house at will. Routinely whipping the kids with his belt for various kinds of offenses, he verbally berated and criticized them day in and day out. He would whack the older kids, especially the boys, with anything that happened to be near his hands—a switch, a flyswatter, a broom handle, or a stick. It didn't seem to matter to him; one would do the job as well as the other. He was a big, angry, drunken man, and he kept every member of his household terrified whenever he was around. Every one of them had learned to jump at his commands.

The kids lived in such fear of ending up on the receiving end of one of his drunken rages that they learned to wake one another when they heard him coming home late at night. Grabbing a blanket or a coat or something else to throw on the ground as bedding, they'd run outside to stay out in the brush until he stopped cursing and plundering around the house and finally fell asleep. On occasion he would punish them the next day for running out, but the kids had learned that punishment administered when he was sober was usually much less severe than what he meted out when he was drunk.

The pattern of wandering and drunkenness Luther had gotten used to over the years became a habit he was never able to break away from. There got to be occasions, for example, when he would just go off and leave the family, usually for only a day or so but sometimes for weeks or even months, without saying a word about where he was going, what he was going to do, or when he would be back. He behaved this way off and on for the rest of his life, ignoring the destructive effects what he was doing had on Pirley and their kids.

His absences were typically nothing more than drunken binges, from which he'd come back after a while, spouting insincere apologies for having been away so long. Upon his return, Pirley would at once vent her rage over the misery he'd caused her and the kids, after which they would roar off into a whole new round of blaring argumentation and fighting. Later, once they managed to make up, they'd head out together once again, always for more of the drinking and partying they enjoyed so much. Without a ripple, their past pattern of behavior would then resume, as if Luther had never been away. It was a crazy and non-sensical way to live, but that's what they did.

*****

For reasons that he made no effort to explain or justify, Luther would on occasion come home all inspired and excited about moving away, always to a new town he just knew would be a much better place for their family to live. Whenever this happened, he and Pirley would once again load up all their meager belongings, gather up the kids, and head out for the new location, the new town that was to be their salvation but, of course, never was.

Typically, the new location would be unknown to any of them but Luther, who wouldn't name it until they arrived on the spot. Until they got there, other members of the family had no idea where they would be living. Always wrongly believing that greener pastures and more fertile valleys would be found someplace else, he did the same again and again, keeping every member of his household at loose ends and upset nearly all the time.

Their moves normally came up unexpectedly, often on a weekend or during a holiday, which was the best timing for relocation by people who owed large amounts of back rent or utility bills or grocery bills or whatever. And, since they never knew where they were going until they got there, it was never possible for any member of the family to leave a forwarding address or let anyone know where they were going. If any member of the family asked how they could stay in touch with a friend or acquaintance, they were told to either send a letter with no return address or to make pay phone calls that none of them could afford. For this reason, normal friendships were impossible to keep.

The so-called *homes* Luther settled his family in became worse and worse with every move, until he finally had his family living in old buildings that were nothing more than rundown shacks. All too often, they were paint-bare, unsafe, abandoned structures that could be squatted in without being spotted by a property owner who cared enough to run them off. Once, during a stretch when he was unable to find even as much as an abandoned building, they lived in a cement drainage pipe under a highway, just to have some shelter from the elements.

Near the end of their years together, the Caines lived in buildings that had no access to electricity or running water. Instead, they used water out of storage containers Luther filled at night from anywhere he could find a spigot. They used a scrap wood burning stove for heating and cooking. Their toilets were thrown-together outhouses he set up in fields or backyards outside where they were living. They got their clothing and furniture from secondhand stores, Salvation Army outlets, charitable drop-off points, or local dumps, and they lived off public relief and handouts in combination with any income he brought home from whatever paid work he could find. Life was miserable for every member of the household, but it was especially disorienting and awful for the kids.

Pirley and the kids had learned that it was best to toe the line when dealing with Luther, since they lived in fear of his irrational behavior. They knew that he could and most definitely would do harm to any one of them if he got upset over something they said or did, especially when he got off into one of his drunken tirades. In Pirley's case, it could happen even when she was pregnant or after she had just delivered, and she was in one or the other of those states most of the time. When he got upset about something, he was likely to beat her up or whip the kids with his belt. He terrorized all of them; wife and kids alike.

*****

As the years ground slowly by, Pirley, who had never been much of a role model anyway, ended up becoming just as irresponsible as Luther. She gave up on any pretense of trying to run a functional household or for acting like a real mother. In effect, she became just like her husband, a person who took her pleasure wherever and whenever she could find it, without paying much attention to any adverse consequences her behavior had on their kids. Because there was no happiness was to be found in her dismal household, she grasped at any opportunity that arose to get out and have some fun. Because she was desperate, she behaved in desperate ways. She ended up becoming a woman who routinely caroused, boozed, and carried on in ways most anyone would have described as wanton and promiscuous. Whether she really did fall to those levels or not is something only she could say.

As Pirley's increasingly dissolute behavior combined with her already irritable and argumentative personality, she became mouthier than ever, and that, as would be imagined, enraged Luther more than ever. Pirley's own behavior had convinced him that she deserved every stroke of *discipline* he meted out, and he made sure she knew it, whereupon their relationship grew stormier with every passing day. Irresponsible behavior begat even more irresponsible behavior, until they found themselves locked into a cycle of abuse neither of them had any idea how to break out of.   After that, there was no going back.

Why did Luther and Pirley always have so much trouble getting along?   Was it because he resented her having decided that it would be impossible to change him and that her best bet was to give up and join him in his revelries, when he really didn't want her to?   Did he somehow conclude, however wrongly, that she had led him astray and encouraged his reckless lifestyle?   Asking who was most at fault is like trying to figure out which came first, the chicken or the egg.   After the fact, why does it matter, if the result is the same either way?

For a whole host of reasons, their 20-year marriage finally fell apart, just as those who knew them back in their early days had predicted it would. They had been unable to get along for as long as they were together.   Everyone had seen it coming, but they hung in there much longer than anyone expected, even though, in many ways, it would have been better if they hadn't.   In the end, all that really mattered was that every member of their household suffered while they were together—husband, wife, and hapless children alike.

— 36 —

THE BLUE GIRL,
CANDY LEE CAINE

IT IS IMPOSSIBLE not to wonder if Luther and Pirley's children were able to do well after they reached maturity, and, if they did, how they managed to get by. Did they have to deal with all manner of difficulties as they made their way through life? The short answer to every question that might be asked about them, as most people would imagine, is that children who get off to a start like theirs often don't do very well at all. Many of them, in fact, end up having far more problems than they know how to handle.

Worse still, there is an abundance of empirical evidence to show that way too many kids raised like they were, after they reach adulthood and get out on their own, end up replicating the despicable lifestyles of their own abusive parents. As disheartening as this is to contemplate, that's how life works out for lots of them. Like sponges, kids soak up the values, attitudes, views, and habits of those who guide them, even when their guides are as negative as they can be. Role models, whether they are good or bad, have an enormous impact on young people.

When it comes to living happy, productive, stable lives, children brought up without a healthy family structure often fail as adults, sometimes so spectacularly they seem to burst out in flames. Growing up without genuine parental affection, natural love, and ordinary adult guidance can be the hidden cause of behavior so inexplicably self-destructive that it comes across as off-the-wall crazy to others. Damaged young people have been known to do things so patently harmful as to be completely unfathomable.

It is clear to any rational observer that the warped thinking caused by childhood deprivation isn't good for kids, but many of us don't give enough thought to the fact that it isn't good for society either. When children are left to their own devices instead of being shepherded to adulthood by dedicated caregivers, our social system can end up having to pay a very steep price. Conversely, extending a helping hand to young people at times of great need can pay great dividends. These are the flip sides of the same coin.

So, what did happen to the Caine's 12 children after Luther and Pirley untethered all of them from the workaday world? In their innocence, did they end up becoming hapless victims of their parents' thoughtless choices, or did they manage to do well in life, despite having to play against a deck that was stacked against them from the outset? In a world like ours, is it even possible for children forced to endure an ordeal like the one their parents put them through to grow up undamaged and whole?

For fair-minded people who want to live in a just and compassionate society, these are important questions. Children deserve support and guidance that was not there for the Caine kids, back when, in their innocence, they were pushed out into what surely must have felt like a harsh and uncaring world. The kids were bright-eyed and intelligent enough to have done quite well for themselves, if they'd had even half a chance. It is an absolute crying shame that more and better help was not available for them, back when it was sorely needed. The lack of it meant that an enormous amount of human talent and ability was undeveloped and, therefore, wasted.

Knowing how Bonnie Marie Tiger (or "Tiger," as she was called) was raised is necessary to understand why she was drawn to Colonel George Jackson Caine in the first place. "Mock's Bad Stomp," the first in this series three inter-connected books about the Caine family, was written to answer that very question. It is an in-depth explanation of how parents Early and Etta "Mock" (Burnham) Tiger turned their daughter Bonnie into the indifferent mother she turned out to be.

In turn, "The Disgrace of Colonel Caine," the second book in the series, was written to explain why George Caine's son Luther treated his wife and children as terribly as he did, which is a tragedy that cannot be understood without knowing how his parents, George Jackson and Bonnie Marie (Tiger) Caine, raised him. Providing that explanation is what this book has been all about. Without it, it would never be clear how family history repeated itself through multiple generations of Caines.

"The Blue Girl, Candy Lee Caine," the third and final book in the series, is being written to describe what became of Luther and Pirley Caine and their 12 highly unlucky children, which is, in a nutshell, what the entire series has been designed to do. As a means of explaining what happened to all of them in common, one child's progress through life will presented in detail; after that, more information will be added to describe what became of each of the eleven others.

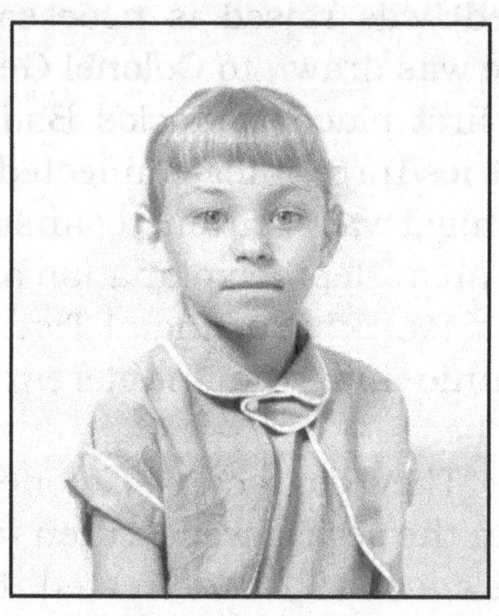

Far too much happened to the Caine children to leave their individual stories unexamined. In the end, the overriding question that begs to be answered is simply this: Were unforgivable crimes and unspeakable injustices committed by or against them?   The denouement of this series of three books, an explanation of what became of each child in turn, was too involved to be included in the immediate narrative, but it will be out in a little while, just as soon as it can be made to happen.

Ω Ω Ω Ω Ω

ALSO BY
MICKEY J. "MIKE" MARTIN

MOCK'S BAD STOMP
ISBN 9780963827975 (Hardback)
ISBN 9780963827982 (Paperback)
ISBN 9780963827999 (EPUB)
LCCN 2021909316

HOFFMAN, OKMULGEE COUNTY, OKLAHOMA: DOING
BUSINESS ON THE INDIAN TERRITORY FRONTIER
ISBN 978-0-9638279-2-0 (Hardback)
LCCN 95060134

BRYANT: A CREEK INDIAN NATION TOWNSITE
ISBN 9780963827913 (Hardback)
ISBN 9781478198956 (Paperback)
LCCN 2012942764

*****

THE LADY LUCK: STORY OF THE USS LST-864
ISBN 9780963827951 (Hardback)
LCCN 2003095571

*****